"My revenge is complete," Slade said mockingly

Taryn went cold, feeling as if a knife had just been plunged into her. "R-revenge?" she repeated with an uncontrollable shiver.

"Mmm. In return for the treatment meted out by you and your brother." He smiled mirthlessly. "It might make you think twice about playing the same trick on some other family in future."

"But I've already told you that I wasn't..." She came to a despairing stop. If he hadn't believed her before, she was only wasting her time attempting to convince him of her innocence now. "Luke said I was a fool for getting involved with you," she recalled bitterly. "Apparently he was right!"

Books by Kerry Allyne

HARLEQUIN ROMANCE

HARLEQUIN PRESENTS

These books may be available at your local bookstore.

Don't miss any of our special offers. Write to us at the following address for information on our newest releases.

Harlequin Reader Service
P.O. Box 52040, Phoenix, AZ 85072-2040
Canadian address: P.O. Box 2800, Postal Station A,
5170 Yonge St., Willowdale, Ont. M2N 6J3

Merringannee Bluff

Kerry Allyne

Harlequin Books

TORONTO • NEW YORK • LONDON
AMSTERDAM • PARIS • SYDNEY • HAMBURG
STOCKHOLM • ATHENS • TOKYO • MILAN

Original hardcover edition published in 1985
by Mills & Boon Limited

ISBN 0-373-02725-7

Harlequin Romance first edition November 1985

CHAPTER ONE

SUNSET COUNTRY! That was the name given to the northwestern corner of the Australian State of Victoria. Also known as 'the Mallee' due to the dense scrub of eucalyptus of the same name that had once covered almost the entire area, but where vast tracts had been cleared so that now it was the State's second largest grain treasury—and as Taryn Rodgers looked out from her parents' truck at the passing fields of gently waving young wheat she hoped it presaged a more prosperous two days in Jinda Jinda, the town they were heading for, than the last three had in Mildura.

Since her grandfather's time the Rodgers family had been carnival people, following the show circuit from town to town all over the country with their novelty and games stalls, but over the last few years the dollar had proved to be very elusive in sideshow alley so, as this was the first time they had decided to try their hand at Jinda Jinda, they were hoping for a change of luck.

However, by early afternoon the following day when the show was getting into full swing, Taryn was beginning to wonder if they had made the right decision after all, for althought the weather was perfect and the crowds good for such a relatively small town, business at both her own stall and her father and brother's shooting gallery a short distance away had been practically non-existent. How her mother was faring with her novelties, etcetera, she had no idea as

her other parent's stall was on the opposite side of the
show ring, but surmising business, or the lack of it,
was probably similar there, she was combing her
fingers somewhat dejectedly through her curling,
shoulder length hair and renewing her practised
spruiking in a rather less anticipatory tone.

'Come on boys and girls, fellers! Roll up, roll up!
Hoop-la . . . three rings for a dollar! Try your luck and
see how easy it is! What about you, madam? Win a
prize for your little girl—she'd love a new doll,' she
smiled encouragingly at a prospective customer
walking by. Then, on receiving a negative shake of the
head from the woman in response, sighed briefly and
continued, 'Come on, folks! It's the pick of the stall! A
box of chocolates, a cuddly toy for the kids, a watch
for yourself! Choose your own prize! It's only three
for a dollar!'

'You mean that? If I win I get to choose what I want?'
an amiable male voice suddenly queried behind her.

'That's what I said, sir. You win—you choose,'
Taryn was already agreeing eagerly even before she
turned to face her enquirer. Not much older than her
own twenty-one years, he was dressed in typical
country garb of fawn drills, short-sided stock boots,
and with a wide bush hat shading a pleasant featured
face wherein a pair of lively hazel eyes showed all too
clearly his appreciation for the delicately heart-shaped
face with its wide curving mouth, darkly fringed
lavender eyes, and crowning red-gold hair now turned
towards him. 'Three for a dollar, that's all! Give it a
try—you won't be disappointed!' she added, giving
him a brilliant smile as she held out three rubber
rings. It wouldn't be the first time her indisputably
good looks had brought in a customer, Taryn knew,
and she wasn't above playing on the fact. Not because

she particularly wanted it that way, nor because it promoted any feeling of vanity. It was merely convenient for business, and business was what they needed right now. Besides, there was also the point to consider that one customer invariably managed to attract others and hopefully this time would be no different.

'In that case I'd be a fool not to give it a whirl, wouldn't I?' the young man grinned, and digging into his hip pocket withdrew five dollars which he handed across to her. 'And five turns should improve my chances even more.'

Pushing the note into the money apron tied about her slim waist, Taryn gave him the required number of rings quickly, happily. Maybe their luck was about to change, after all. 'Sure it will, sir! Sure it will,' she beamed. 'Just get three rings over any item on the board and whatever you fancy is yours.'

A few minutes later, though, and with him well on the way to winning at least three prizes, some of her happiness was starting to be replaced with a little anxiety. It wasn't that she didn't want him to win—a winner was always good for business, as evidenced by the number of people who had stopped to watch and thus were likely prospects themselves—but at the same time if he had too many her stall was going to end up losing money rather than making it, and so she began her sales pitch again in the hope of distracting him a little.

'Over here, folks! Over here! See a winner in action and join him!' she called with a beckoning wave of her arm. 'Who's next? How about you, boys?' to a trio of primary school children. 'This could be your lucky day too! You look as if you'd all have accurate throwing arms!'

For a moment the youngest of the three appeared tempted, but then one of his companions voiced his thoughts on the matter. 'Nah! I'd rather have a hot dog and some candy floss.' And convincing the others they would also, the three of them began drifting away.

Their departure seemed to be a signal for the rest of the onlookers to continue on their ways as well, although one giggling teenage girl did have an unsuccessful try before ambling off with her friends too, leaving Taryn to discover her original customer just concluding his last throw and thereby winning four out of a possible five prizes.

'Well, you certainly appear to be in touch today, sir,' she forced herself to smile, trying to make the best of it. If she hadn't made it the pick of the stall it wouldn't have been quite so bad, but as it was . . . 'So what would you like as your prizes? A watch, I suppose.' It was the best prize they had, despite the fact that it obviously wasn't worth even a quarter of the one he was already wearing. 'And perhaps you'd care for . . .'

'How about a date instead?' he interposed with a friendly grin. 'After all, you did say I could choose whatever prize I fancied.'

Taryn gave an amused half laugh. She'd had customers try to date her before, but never in lieu of something from the stall. 'Except I was meaning whatever prize you fancied from those on display back there.' Indicating the shelves behind the counter.

'I'd still rather take you out,' he smiled.

'Yes, well, that's very nice of you, but I'm afraid you're going to have to select something from the shelves all the same,' she informed him wryly. 'In any event, once we're working a show there's no time for

dating. The evenings are often our busiest times and
the stalls don't usually shut until after eleven.'

'That's no problem. Our show cabaret will only just
be warming up by then,' he laughed. 'So how about it,
hmm? I could collect you here when you shut up for
the night and take you back with me. It's only being
held in the pavilion behind the Members' Stand on
the far side of the ring.'

For a second or two Taryn was tempted. Being on
the move all the time as she usually was didn't allow
her much opportunity for meeting and making friends,
of either sex, and certainly this young man seemed a
lot nicer than some of those who had previously made
advances towards her. Then, with a rueful shaping of
her soft mouth, she shook her head.

'Thanks all the same, but I don't think . . .'

'I plan to stay here until you do agree, you know,'
he interrupted once again, with another of his cheerful
grins.

'But you can't,' she half smiled, half frowned. 'I
have a living to earn, and I can't do that while I'm
talking to you.'

'Then I'll play some more hoop-la while you're
drumming up some other customers,' he proposed,
withdrawing another five dollars from his pocket.

Taryn gave a more vigorous shake of her head this
time, her expression dry. 'At your success rate, I can
afford that even less! I owe you four prizes already.'

'All of which I agree to forfeit, plus any others in
future, provided you say you'll go to the cabaret with
me,' encouragingly.

'That's not fair to you, though,' she protested
helplessly as he pushed the five dollars into her hand
and began helping himself to more rings, 'You can't
keep playing and taking nothing when you win.'

'Why not?' he shrugged indifferently and, taking aim, scored another success. 'That's also my choice, isn't it?' Pausing, he flashed her a roguish grin over one shoulder. 'Besides, maybe this way you'll take pity on me.'

Taryn couldn't help laughing. He was certainly persistent, but in such a way that it was really impossible for her to become irritated. It also had her musing as to whether she should change her mind about accompanying him—exactly as it was obviously meant to do! But he did seem to be very pleasant, and as the apparent venue for the cabaret was hardly any distance from where her family had set up camp, what harm could there possibly be in her accepting his invitation? she asked herself. And especially when she did actually feel like going.

'All right, you win,' she smiled at length. 'I'll go to the cabaret with you.'

'That's great!' His return smile was enthusiastically boyish. 'I'll pick you up here at about eleven, then, shall I?'

'No, you'd better make it half past, and at our van in the camping area, I think,' she amended. 'That will give me time to have a shower and change.'

'Okay,' he nodded equably, the corners of his mouth beginning to tilt with wry humour. 'By the way, just in case you're wondering, I'm Jefferson—Jeff—Douglas.'

'Taryn Rodgers,' she revealed in turn, her own lips curving in response. It was always handy to know just whom one was going out with!

His acknowledgment came in the form of a finger raised to the brim of his hat before half turning and tossing another ring casually, but unsuccessfully, at the hoop-la board. 'And you're only in town for the duration of the show, are you, Taryn?'

'Mmm, we'll be moving on as soon as it's finished. We heard there's a rodeo to be held at Linwood in a couple of days so we thought we'd give it a try there. We've never been through this part of Victoria before so we're more or less feeling our way at the moment, just to see how it goes and whether it's worthwhile returning next year,' she explained.

Jeff nodded. 'I thought I hadn't seen you before. I'm sure I would have remembered you if I had,' with an admiring glance. 'You must get to see a tremendous amount of the country, though, travelling round the whole time.'

'Oh, yes, we definitely do that,' she averred, pulling a somewhat wry face.

'You don't like moving all the time?' he hazarded.

She partly lifted one shoulder diffidently. 'Mostly I do, although there are occasions when you think it would be nice just to stay in one place for a little longer than a few days, of course, but at least it's not so bad now that we've finished school.'

'We?' His brows rose enquiringly.

'My younger brother and myself.' She halted, her expression becoming reminiscent. 'It used to be lousy being the new kids in school wherever we went, but Mum always insisted that in conjunction with our correspondence lessons we should also attend whatever school was available as well, so it would be a day or two at this one and half a day at that one all the time. It wasn't a particularly easy way to learn but we did our best to stick at it because it obviously meant so much to Mum. I'm not sorry that we did now—it's really only when you've left school that you realise how important it is—but at the same time I didn't have any regrets when it was finally all behind me either,' she laughed on an eloquent note. Then, 'But how about you? Have you lived in Jinda Jinda all your life?'

Jeff tossed another ring in the general direction of one of the board's targets as he answered. 'Actually we don't live in Jinda Jinda at all. We live about forty miles or so out of town.'

'We?' It was Taryn's arching brows that peaked now.

'My mother, older brother, and myself,' he advised. 'Dad died in a tractor accident about ten years ago so there's just the three of us now.'

Her features clouded sympathetically. 'I'm sorry. Although from that I gather you live on a property.' And after his confirming nod, 'Wheat?'

'And sheep.' He started to laugh. 'Plus the dogs, of course.'

'The dogs?' Her head angled quizzically.

'Mmm, my brother breeds them—Australian sheep dogs, pedigree kelpies—and extremely successfully too, I might add. They're very sought after, the Merringannee breed, both in this country and overseas. In fact, he's already sold four young ones here this morning. The demand for good working dogs is unbelievable.'

'I'm not surprised,' said Taryn. Many times she had seen kelpies at work in the outback and knew just how much they were capable of accomplishing. 'A good one means a great deal to a grazier, doesn't it?'

'My word it does!' Jeff's agreement was emphatic. 'Properly trained, they can do the work of six men when mustering and yarding, and they make sheep on a vast scale in huge paddocks and often under harsh conditions economically possible.'

'I've also heard they're . . .' She broke off, her lips twitching whimsically, on seeing a familiar figure about to join them. She had wondered how long it would be before either her father or her brother put in an appearance. One of them always did when they noticed a male customer remaining at her stall for any length of time. It was her father's way of protecting her from any possible hassles with troublemakers or unwanted admirers, as well as the reason why he always arranged for their stalls to be sited not too far apart.

'Hi! Everything going okay? No troubles?' her brother now asked as he came to a halt beside her. At eighteen he was only a couple of inches taller than Taryn's five foot six, his denim-clad frame slender and wiry rather than muscular, his reddish brown hair long, his blue gaze quick and alert.

'No, everything's fine,' she hastened to assure him, smiling. And to the older of the two, 'This is my brother, Luke, Jeff. Jeff Douglas,' she completed for her relative's benefit. Adding, after their casual acknowledgments, 'Jeff's taking me to the show cabaret after we finish tonight.'

'Oh?' Luke's eyes widened a little in surprise at her obviously unanticipated information. 'That's the one that's being held in the pavilion over there, isn't it?' Nodding his head towards the other side of the show ring. 'When I heard about it I thought I might see what it's like myself.'

'Everyone's welcome,' inserted Jeff genially. 'And most years it gets the nod as having been a very successful and enjoyable evening.'

Luke shrugged offhandedly. 'Yeah, well, if there's nothing else doing I might give it a go. Dancing's not really my scene. I'd rather get up a game of cards.' He paused, glancing up at Jeff enquiringly. 'I don't suppose you'd care for a few hands, would you? Sam

Cowper and I have got a game going at the moment down in the camping area.'

'But I thought you were supposed to be helping Dad,' cut in Taryn before her companion could answer.

Luke sent a meaningful look in their father's direction. 'I hardly think he needs me to help him with a grand total of two customers,' he grimaced mockingly. 'In any event, that's why I'm back now—just to keep an eye on how things are going.' He turned back to Jeff. 'Well, how about it? Do you feel like sitting in for a while? It's only a friendly game with a two-dollar limit.'

Jeff seemed to give the idea some amenable thought. 'What are you playing . . . euchre?'

'Uh-uh! Jack-high poker.'

'Okay, I'll be in that, then,' came the ready acceptance.

'But you can't,' interjected Taryn. 'Not only haven't you finished your turns here, but . . .' with a partly exasperated, partly anxious glance that encompassed both of them, 'you know very well that it's against the law, anyhow.'

'And you know very well that it's done all the time,' countered Luke in dry tones. 'So what the law doesn't know, doesn't hurt them, and as I said, it is only a friendly game, after all.'

A remark which had his sister eyeing him dubiously. On occasion it had been known for Luke to arrive home with a considerable amount of winnings from some of his so-called *friendly* games, and although she knew he was a good player, just sometimes she couldn't prevent feelings of doubt creeping in that he was so skilful as to very rarely lose.

'While as for my unfinished turns here,' Jeff broke

in on her concerned thoughts lightly, 'you can have them for me. I've already won what I wanted.' And as he started to move off with her brother, 'If I don't see you again beforehand, I'll meet you at your caravan at eleven-thirty, right?'

Accepting what appeared to be the inevitable, Taryn sighed and smiled faintly. 'It's the big white one next to the green truck and the blue ute with a trailer.'

'Don't worry, I'll point it out to him while we're down there,' said Luke over his shoulder as he led the way.

Taryn watched them with her lower lip caught between pearly white teeth until they were out of sight. It wasn't exactly that she doubted her brother's basic honesty, but he was only young and easily led. And particularly by someone like Sam Cowper whose family operated a hot dog and drinks stall, and who more than once had involved Luke in some, what could only have been called, questionable ventures. Ventures that had, once or twice, brought police investigation, even though nothing had actually been proven, she recalled with disquiet. It was just that Luke had a tendency to be lazy and, therefore, any get-rich-quick scheme immediately appealed to him, she supposed.

For the remainder of the afternoon Taryn's apprehensive musings continued along much the same lines. Mainly because she hated to think that by having become friendly with Jeff Douglas she may have inadvertently involved him in something it would have been better for him to avoid—if indeed her brother's friendly card school wasn't quite as reputable as it could have been!

Fortunately, however, as the sinking sun gave a breathtaking display, confirming the area's Sunset

Country appellation, and the mingling crowds began to increase considerably for the evening's entertainment both in the ring and sideshow alley, her stall became sufficiently well patronised to relegate such uneasy thoughts to the back of her mind as she concentrated all her efforts on swelling her day's takings.

By the time the show had closed for the evening, though, and she had showered and changed from her customary jeans and shirt into a black velvet skirt which she teamed with a black, scooped-neck and long-sleeved, fine wool top—although warm by day, in October the Mallee could still be quite cold at night—her misgivings had returned and she awaited Jeff's arrival restively. If she had only been able to have a word with Luke she would have felt less tense, Taryn was sure, but as neither she nor her mother or father had set eyes on him since earlier in the day, even that hopeful reassurance had been denied her.

When he did arrive, however, Jeff appeared to be in the same carefree good spirits as he had been when she first met him, much to Taryn's relief, but none the less, as soon as she had introduced him to her parents and they were heading across the showgrounds she just had to bring up the matter that had occupied her thoughts for so much of the day.

'So how was the card game?' she began as nonchalantly as possible. 'Did you win?'

'Only occasionally,' he half laughed, half grimaced. 'Lord! I thought I knew my cards but that brother of yours and his mate are something else again. I've never seen such hands as they held.'

Taryn's heart sank in dismay. 'You lost, then?' she gulped.

'I guess you could say that,' he owned ruefully, and

then gave an expressive laugh. 'Slade put it rather more bluntly.'

'Slade?' she queried hesitantly.

'My brother.' His elucidation was accompanied by a graphic expression. 'Not that I suppose I can altogether blame him for erupting as he did,' he went on in a drily humorous voice. 'It was his money I lost.'

'Oh, no!' Taryn exclaimed worriedly. 'I'm so sorry.'

'Whatever for?' Jeff smiled down at her quizzically. 'It wasn't your fault. I should have known better than to play with his money in the first place.'

Unhappily, his forbearance didn't make her feel any better and she began chewing at her lip again. 'Well, it was really through me that you got into the game, and—and . . .' She faltered to a stop, feeling worse by the minute. 'Did you—lose much?'

He gave a dismissive shrug. 'No, not really. Only a couple of hundred. With luck like that Sam has it could have been a lot worse, I guess.'

In the midst of silently gasping over the amount, Taryn abruptly cast him a searching glance from beneath thick, curling lashes. Had she imagined it, or had there been some pointed emphasis in that last comment? 'M-meaning?' she forced out fearfully.

'Only that I wish I'd had his cards instead of the ones I did have,' he laughed off her question negligently.

Taryn breathed a sigh of relief and thought it best not to press the matter any further. If he wasn't already suspicious of the circumstances surrounding his loss, she might unintentionally make him so by pursuing the subject, and to date she still really couldn't be certain that Luke and his friend had done anything wrong anyway!

They could hear the sound of the band in the

pavilion long before they reached the building and as they approached the steps leading inside, and the sound grew in proportion, Jeff glanced down with a smile.

'I told you they'd only just be warming up by now, didn't I? This will go on for hours yet. The town always treats itself to a rage on show night.'

'So I see,' chuckled Taryn as they skirted a couple by the doorway before entering the main hall which was a kaleidoscope of colour as dancing couples whirled when they could, but more often shuffled, around the densely crowded floor. 'By the look of it the whole of the town's population must be here.'

'More than likely,' he conceded in between acknowledging greetings from many of the people they passed. 'Together with all those from the outlying districts as well, of course.' He inclined his head towards the dancers. 'Shall we join them?'

'We may as well,' she grinned, already beginning to enjoy herself. The enthusiasm and evident pleasure of those already participating was contagious.

For a while they made their way around the floor as best they could in silence, the band making it almost impossible to conduct any sort of conversation, but as they once more headed away from the dais where the musicians were zestfully beating out their fervent rhythm, Taryn again felt able to voice a question without having to shout.

'Where does one sit when not dancing?' she asked interestedly. There weren't any seats around the edge of the hall that she could see, but she couldn't imagine some of the older couples present being prepared, or in some cases even able, to stand all evening.

In reply Jeff nodded towards that side of the building they hadn't yet passed. 'There's another room through that doorway over there. That's where the bar is too.'

Taryn nodded. 'I'd like to have that concession for the night. With this crowd I bet they do a roaring trade.'

'They certainly were when I was in there last,' he endorsed. 'Would you care for something cold to drink yourself?'

'Ten minutes ago I would have said no, but now . . . yes, please,' she assented with heartfelt eloquence.

'Okay, then, just stick close and we'll see if we can make it.'

As it happened, it took them quite a number of minutes to weave and manoeuvre their laughing way across to the appropriate doorway, and on reaching it they almost fell through the opening as they squeezed themselves out of the crush on the other side. Here, there were a number of tables and chairs conveniently set out, Taryn noted. Most of those at the far end of the room occupied by an extremely elegantly dressed group who all appeared to be included in one particular party of people. Nearer to the door was the bar, its length as heavily besieged as she had envisaged on such a well-attended occasion, and it was in this direction that they began to drift as soon as they had recovered their breath.

Before they could reach it, however, a tall, exceptionally built man of some thirty-two years, and dressed in the most beautifully tailored dark green suit Taryn had ever seen suddenly detached himself from the party at the other end of the room and began striding purposefully between the intervening tables. For some unknown reason, Taryn immediately sensed that it was Jeff and herself rather than a desire to patronise the bar that had brought him to his feet, and as a result she watched his approach curiously, covertly, from the corner of her eye.

What with his nearly coal black hair and equally dusky framed, dark grey eyes set in a strong manly face, he was definitely one good-looking hunk, was her initial, quite involuntary assessment. His mouth was wide and firm but with a hint of a quirk, despite its being drawn into a more forbidding line at the moment, his jaw lean and square, and taut now as if from a rigid control being exercised. He carried himself erectly, with authority, and she felt intuitively that there was a strength in him, a tough resilience, coupled with an iron resolve of will that would make him a steadfast and indomitable ally, but an utterly devastating foe.

With only the barest of cool glances in her direction on reaching them, he promptly addressed himself to Jeff in a low, impatient voice. 'Where the hell did you disappear to?' he demanded. 'We do have guests here, you know . . . that you're supposed to be helping to entertain!'

Jeff executed a deprecating shrug. 'Oh, come on, Slade!' he exhorted good-naturedly. 'They can entertain themselves here by dancing, surely. Besides . . .' he smiled down at Taryn and, dropping an arm about her shoulders, drew her closer, 'I've got someone of my own to entertain. That's also why I went missing . . . in order to pick her up.' Looking down at the girl next to him again, his mouth curved obliquely. 'In case you haven't already guessed, this is my brother, Slade.' And to the older man, 'Taryn Rodgers. My date for the evening.'

'Rodgers!' Slade immediately repeated on a rough and somewhat disbelieving note before Taryn even had a chance to acknowledge the introduction. 'You don't mean to tell me she's connected to that thieving card-sharp who robbed you blind this afternoon! For God's sake, Jeff, I thought you had more sense! What's her part in tonight's proceedings ... to inveigle you into another game so they can relieve you of even more cash?'

Taryn's face flamed, but it was her escort who answered first. 'Oh, of course not!' he retorted in mild exasperation. 'I'd already asked Taryn for a date before I met her brother. My playing cards with him had nothing to do with her.'

'You mean, that once having hooked you with a pretty face,' a raking, disparaging glance was thrown Taryn's way, 'she didn't then conveniently introduce you to him?'

'Well—yes—she introduced us ... but only incidentally,' Jeff finished in a rush on seeing the contemptuous curl that began catching at the edges of his brother's mouth. 'He just happened to join us while I was at her stall, that's all.'

'In response to a pre-arranged signal from her, no doubt! She catches them—he fleeces them!' Slade bit out in savagely scornful tones.

'That's not true!' Taryn spoke up for herself now, furiously. How dared he make such an odious conjecture! If she couldn't even be certain her brother didn't win honestly, then how could he be so positive Jeff had been cheated? While as for claiming she was also involved ... well, that was just the last straw! 'You have no basis for contending any such thing! There's no proof that my brother was running a crooked game, and ...'

'No proof?' Slade interjected derisively. 'You may have managed to convince my brother of that, honey, but thankfully I'm not so gullible! Of course the game was crooked! Any bloody fool would know that after hearing a description of the events that took place!'

'That's still only supposition ... not proof!' she maintained valiantly, despite her own doubts on the matter. It *was* her brother he was denigrating when all was said and done. 'And for your information, I didn't encourage Jeff to play—just the opposite, in fact—I tried to stop him.'

'In the hopes of making more money for yourself out of him at your stall, huh?'

'No!' she gritted irately, her hand just itching to slap that jeering look from his handsome face. 'Primarily, because it's against the law, if you must know!'

He laughed at that, sarcastically, but before he could speak Jeff came to her aid. 'That's true, Slade,' he tried impressing on him. 'Taryn didn't really want Luke or me to play.'

'Probably because it sounds better for their marks,' proposed Slade caustically, still obviously unconvinced. 'It wouldn't look so good if she was too eager to get them involved, would it?'

Jeff shook his head despairingly. 'You're wrong, old son, totally wrong, you know. At least where Taryn's concerned, at any rate. I was there, you weren't, and I *know* she wasn't implicated ... in any way,' he concluded decisively.

His brother uttered another laugh, a mocking half one this time. 'Lord, you've really let a pair of amethyst eyes and a practised air of innocence take you in, haven't you? How much is it going to cost you this evening, I wonder?'

'Okay, that's enough, Slade! I didn't bring Taryn here to be insulted by you! So just give it a rest, will you?' Jeff ordered rather than requested, his own voice sharpening now. 'If you can't accept her for what she is ...'

'Oh, but I do,' inserted Slade silkily. Too silkily in Taryn's estimation. 'Unfortunately, it appears to be only you who isn't able to do so.'

'Then you know exactly what you can ...'

'No!' It was Taryn who broke in on this occasion as she placed an arresting hand on her companion's arm, a faint smile of gratitude for his defence of her shaping her soft lips. It was all too apparent nothing was going to alter his brother's opinion of her, but as she had no wish to cause more dissension between them ... 'I think it might be best if I just left,' she murmured placatingly.

'Sounds like the best suggestion I've heard all evening,' put in Slade grimly, but by doing so had her anger rapidly escalating again.

'That doesn't surprise me in the slightest!' she rounded on him in scathing tones. 'Because as far as I'm concerned, anyone who put any suggestion to you, other than to leave your arrogant and offensive company, could only be scraping the bottom of the barrel!' And with a proud lifting of her fiery head she about-faced and went storming towards the doorway leading into the main hall, where Jeff caught up to her a few seconds later.

'I'm sorry about that.' His apology was sincerely made. 'It just never occurred to me that Slade would take it into his head to blame you as well for what happened this afternoon. But please don't leave just yet. I'll make sure we don't run into him again.'

Taryn half shrugged in a gesture that was neither an affirmation nor a refusal. 'I don't want to be the cause of any more arguments between the two of you,' she sighed.

'No sweat, you won't be,' he reassured her blithely. 'We've had our differences before and managed to get over them without too much trouble, so if that's all you're worried about, forget it.'

'But what about your guests he mentioned?' she still felt obliged to ask. 'Shouldn't you really be with them? He seemed to think you should.'

'Mmm, but then he didn't realise at the time that you were my guest too.' He bent his head closer. 'And I know who I'd rather spend the evening with.'

'But won't he just keep insisting you join them if he sees I haven't left, after all?' With a rather wary look towards the tables at the far end of the room as if expecting to see Slade bearing down on them once more.

'Hmm . . . he could do, at that,' Jeff conceded in a thoughtful vein. Suddenly his demeanour brightened. 'Then why don't we just split altogether and go somewhere else?'

'Such as?' Taryn's expression turned wry. 'Since you reckoned the whole town was probably here tonight, just where else would there be to go?'

His hazel eyes crinkled with rueful laughter at his own forgetfulness. 'You're right, of course. There won't be anywhere else open, and especially not at this hour.' He lifted his shoulders in a fatalistic gesture. 'Then as I said originally, I guess I'll just have to ensure we don't meet up with him again. It shouldn't be too difficult in this crowd.'

Nevertheless, it soon became apparent that it wasn't quite so easy to lose themselves amongst the other dancers as Jeff envisaged, for after only one slow circuit around the floor it appeared that someone as determined as Slade found it a relatively simple matter to locate them as soon as he and his tall, dark blonde partner joined the dancing.

'I thought you were leaving,' was his first peremptory, condemning comment to Taryn as he closed with the younger couple.

'I changed my mind,' she threw back at him defiantly, taking exception to both his remark and the smirking expression on his companion's haughty face. It had never been her intention to leave merely because he had made it obvious he didn't want her there!

Slade's eyes hardened noticeably, but his next words were directed towards his brother. 'While you do still have responsibilities to fulfil ... whether they fit in with your new plans or not,' he reminded in a grim undertone. 'I can tell you, Mother isn't exactly impressed with your behaviour this evening.'

'So when is she?' quipped Jeff drily, and to Taryn's surprise saw that humorous quirk to Slade's firmly shaped mouth come into play in response. Then it was gone as rapidly as it had appeared.

'That's as may be,' Slade granted in the same incisive voice as before. 'But it doesn't alter the facts. You know damned well what you're supposed to be doing, what you're expected to be doing, so I suggest you get on and do it ... right now!' With which arbitrary directive, plus a last censuring glance at Taryn, he and his partner began moving away.

'Oh, hell!' Jeff expelled a long remorseful breath. 'It looks as if I'm not going to get any peace at all until I do put in at least some sort of effort.' His gaze met Taryn's contritely. 'I'm sorry, but I didn't really expect him to be quite so adamant about it. Mother, yes, but not Slade as well.'

'The latter, I suspect, because your brother clearly doesn't like, or approve, of *me*,' put in Taryn wryly.

'Only because he doesn't really know you and he

seems to have got this fixation about you having been in league with Luke,' he was swift to assure.

Diverted momentarily, she gazed up at him quizzically. 'Do you also believe the same as he does, Jeff? That Luke was running a crooked game?' she asked quietly, reluctantly, but feeling it was imperative she know his true thoughts on the matter.

For a time he was silent, and then he sighed, 'I've got to admit I had my suspicions. Luke and his mate's run of luck was really just too incredible to be true. I mean, when the same two fellers manage to avoid betting against each other every time one of them has the winning hand has to indicate something's going on, even if you can't pick them giving signals.'

'I see,' she nodded despondently. 'Then I'm truly sorry I was the one to get you involved in it, however indirectly, although . . .' a sudden thought occurred, 'I still can't quite understand why, if there was only a two-dollar limit as Luke said, you managed to lose as much as you did. Or even why you didn't drop out immediately you suspected something was amiss, if it comes to that.'

'Yes, well . . .' His lips curved crookedly. 'It may only have been a two-dollar betting limit, but the house rules allowed for raising to whatever was in the centre, and that has the result of lifting an—umm—friendly game into a decidedly heavier bracket. As for the other . . . well, I suppose it's human nature to want to continue playing in the hope of recouping at least some of your losses. That is, until you finally realise you're having yourself on and that all you're doing is throwing good money after bad. Then you do quit.'

Taryn chewed at her lip disconsolately, feeling terrible about it all. Not only because of the amount Jeff had lost—even though from his earlier attitude when he had dismissed it so negligently, and judging by the company his family kept, it was more than evident they were far from the poverty line—but also, and definitely more so, because it had come about at her brother's hands. And for which she resolved to have words with him at the earliest opportunity!

'I'm sorry,' she said again. Then, on suddenly finding herself on the receiving end of a distinctly uncompromising grey gaze from across the room, her thoughts summarily returned to her partner's latest predicament. 'Right at present, though, I somehow think you're likely to lose more than money—like, your head, for instance—if you don't soon make a move to do as your brother decreed, because I just got another look from him that boded no good for either of us.' Her advice was relayed with an expressive grimace.

Following a swift check in his brother's direction, Jeff seemed to come to the same conclusion. 'Mmm, you could be right,' he owned on a droll note. Followed hurriedly by an earnest, 'Look, I really feel badly about having to desert you like this, but I'll tell you what I'll do. I'll introduce you to a few friends of mine from here in town so you will at least have company while I'm gone, and I'll be back in no more than fifteen minutes.' He paused. 'Unless, of course, you'd care to come with me and join the party.'

'Uh-uh! No, thanks!' Taryn declined with a graphic shake of her head. 'I doubt your brother would be in favour of that for a start, and as a result it could prove to be extremely embarrassing for everyone. Also, I think I'll give your offer a miss too, if you don't mind. I think I'd rather take in a breath of fresh air outside instead while I'm waiting. It's becoming markedly warm in here.'

He accepted her decision compliantly. 'While I never did get you that drink, did I? Would you like me to get one for you now?'

'No, thanks all the same. I'll survive,' she smiled as they reached the edge of the dance floor. 'Perhaps we can have one together when you've done your duty.'

'As good as done,' he promised. 'So where will I find you . . . outside?'

'Either there, or somewhere near the doorway, I expect.' One thing was for certain, there was no way she would be taking a seat and waiting for him in the same room that held his brother!

'Okay, I'll see you in a quarter of an hour, then. You can count on it! Just don't go finding yourself another escort in the meantime, hmm? They're a risky lot round here,' he added jokingly.

'I'll keep that in mind,' she retorted in the same bantering fashion as they each went their separate ways.

Outside the pavilion the sky was ablaze with a myriad twinkling stars, the air crisp, although it was a while before Taryn began to notice the chill, and then only for a short time as she promptly disregarded it again on seeing the very person she wanted to speak to nearing the building.

'Luke! I've been wanting to have a word with you,' she began immediately her brother was within talking distance.

'Oh? What about?' he enquired offhandedly. Then went on before she could explain, 'Where's Jeff? You certainly picked a good one for yourself there, didn't you?' The last on a somewhat sly, approving note.

'So did you, by all accounts!' she returned sharply, disliking the connotation he appeared to be placing on her association with her escort.

'Meaning?' His voice stiffened.

She drew a deep breath and plunged on. 'That there are some who are of the opinion that your game of cards wasn't exactly on the level.'

'Including Jeff?'

'As a matter of fact, yes.'

'Oh, now I get it,' he snorted scornfully. 'Just because he lost he's been whining in your ear claiming it was all a set-up, has he?'

'No, he has not!' she denied hotly. 'In fact, all things considered, I think he's taken it very well. He didn't even mention he'd had suspicions about the game until I actually put it to him.'

'*You* put it to him!' Luke echoed, staring at her incredulously. 'And why in blazes would you be suggesting something like that to him? Are you trying to get us into trouble with the cops, or something?'

'Hardly!' Taryn's retort was part sardonically, part angrily made. 'And nor did I *suggest* it to him either. I didn't need to! If he hadn't already had his own suspicions, then the allegations his brother had made—including the rotten surmise that I was implicated in it too!—would certainly have given him sufficient reason to begin thinking along those lines long before I got around to mentioning anything about it!'

'The bastard!' he burst out with unexpected intensity. 'It's always the same with his type! Just because they as good as own the town they think their word is law and that they can accuse everyone else of whatever they please!'

'What do you mean ... own the town?' Taryn frowned, her eyes darkening with confusion. 'The Douglases don't live in Jinda Jinda, they live some distance out of town. Are you sure we're talking about the same people?'

'Yeah, we're talking about the same ones, all right!' Luke insisted. 'The Douglases! True blue members of the Establishment with a capital E, the much-vaunted squattocracy—that's who you've just had a run-in with! The same family that apparently owns just about everything and anything worth owning round here . . . and as far as you can see in any direction. Oh, true, Jeff and this brother of his you met may not live in town, but from what I've heard they have plenty of aunts, uncles, cousins, etcetera, who certainly do. All of whom just about make it impossible to move in Jinda Jinda without one of them knowing about it.'. Halting, he thrust his hands into the front pockets of his jeans, his fervent outburst abating to a more muted resentment. 'Huh! With all they've got, here they are kicking up a fuss over a measly couple of hundred bucks. As if that much means anything to them. Not like it does to us—petrol and food to get us to the next town.'

For a time Taryn was too startled to even comment. Admittedly, at the moment her own feelings towards one particular member of the Douglas family were pretty incensed too, but obviously nowhere to the extent her brother's were. And that surprised her, because she had never even suspected he harboured such thoughts about others who happened to be wealthier than their own family was. Granted, it had been evident for a while now—much to their parent's disappointment—that Luke had an aversion to actually putting in any physical effort with regard to work, preferring instead to earn what money he could by wheeling and dealing whenever possible, or gambling as he had today—the more so since he'd teamed up with Sam Cowper, she now recalled—but it had still come as a shock for her to discover just how resentful he appeared to have become. In consequence, when she did speak, it was in a quiet and careful manner.

'Whether the actual money meant anything to them—which I don't really believe it did—isn't the point, Luke. It's whether it was lost fair and square ... or dishonestly.' She hesitated, unsure whether to wait for him to comment now, or whether to continue. When no response other than a brief hunching of his shoulders was forthcoming, she pressed on. 'So if the game was on the level, how come you and Sam held such good cards and apparently came out the only winners? Didn't *anyone* else in the school get good cards too?'

'How should I know?' he countered touchily. 'I didn't get to see their cards till the end of each hand. Maybe they just kept throwing out the wrong ones. Half of them wouldn't know the makings of a good hand, anyway.'

'But Jeff claimed he did know his cards,' she put forward warily.

'And maybe he does,' he allowed indifferently. 'And maybe he just didn't have any luck today. It's not my fault if he didn't draw the cards he needed. Or perhaps Sam and I are just better players!' His voice began to rise again. 'So what did he expect? For us to let him win because a Douglas did us the honour of sitting in the game? Well, no one twisted his arm in order to make him do so, it was his own decision, and as far as I'm concerned that's all there is to it! He lost! So what?'

Taryn couldn't decide whether he was deliberately avoiding the real issue or not. 'So was the game honest, or wasn't it? That's, so what!' she came out with it flatly. 'After all, there have been similar accusations in other towns, haven't there, Luke?'

'None of which were proven!' he was quick to remind, triumphantly. 'Or have you become so infatuated with the feller because he condescended to notice you that you now believe his word against that of your own brother?'

'Neither, as it so happens!' A touch of acrimony began creeping in to Taryn's own voice now. First, she had been accused by Slade, and now her brother was doing the same in reverse! 'I've defended you every time the matter's been raised, but at the same time, before I can take anybody's word against yours, it would be helpful if I knew just what your word is, because you haven't yet told me!'

'Because it didn't occur to me that you trusted me so little that I'd have to!'

'In other words, you're saying it was fair, is that it?'

'What else?' he abruptly laughed sardonically. 'Sam and I aren't exactly what you'd call novices, you know. We can run rings round just about anyone at cards.'

But individually, or in partnership? the unbidden thought leapt into Taryn's mind, and she had to determinedly expel it. Now she was the one who wasn't being fair when he'd as good as said the game had been above board. After all, she had never known him to lie to her before, and there was such a thing as family loyalty to be considered too.

'Well, if that's all you wanted to see me about, I think I'll be going inside now for a look,' Luke broke in on her reverie in a more normal tone. 'You coming?'

'I suppose so,' she half smiled, gauging Jeff's fifteen minutes to be about up anyhow, and in a mood of better accord brother and sister entered the building together.

CHAPTER TWO

DURING the following, and last day of the show, the ring was even more utilised than it had been the day before, with various classes of sheep and horse judging, trotting races, dressage events and show-jumping, as well as an assortment of other entertainments for both children and adults taking place.

The extra activity brought an even greater attendance with it, but to Taryn's disappointment not very many people visited the sideshow concourse—probably because, it being such a small town, for most of those present it was their second attendance in as many days—and as a result by mid-afternoon her takings were distinctly insignificant. The amusement rides a little distance away were faring slightly better, she noted, but that was little consolation to see when she knew her father's shooting gallery was attracting as little custom as her own stall was, and for the remainder of the afternoon her expression reflected her troubled inner thoughts. If the evening proved to be as unrewarding, then once again there would be no chance of them being in a position to purchase the new set of tyres the truck increasingly needed.

It was nearly six o'clock, and the light beginning to fade, before she saw Jeff for the first time that day. At least for the first time since he had walked her back to her family's caravan in the early hours of the morning, that was!

'Hi! I'm sorry I've been unable to get round to seeing you before this, but since I did more or less

33

promise to be on hand I've been caught up with our guests all day. There's about thirty of them in all so I couldn't very well leave Slade and Mother to handle them on their own again, but neither did I want you to leave without our at least having said goodbye, so I made an excuse to disappear for a while and here I am,' he explained with a smile. 'How have things been going with you?'

'Slowly ... *very* slowly,' she advised, her accompanying grimace expressive. 'But more often than not that seems to be the way of it these days, I'm afraid. People just can't afford to be so free with their money any more.'

'No, I suppose not,' he nodded sympathetically. 'Do you think you'll be back next year, then?'

'I couldn't really say at present,' she shrugged. 'I guess it all depends on our finances at the time. Mum and Dad might prefer to resume following our usual route.'

'I see.' Pausing, he extracted some money from the back pocket of his trousers. 'Well, at least I can do something to help improve your chances of returning by having another few turns now.'

Taryn refused the proferred money with a shake of her head. 'Only if you take the prizes you've already won,' she stipulated with a rueful half laugh. 'Otherwise I wouldn't be at all surprised if I didn't have your brother down here accusing me of trying to cheat you again.' She halted, her expression earnest as her lavender eyes sought and held his. 'Which Luke claimed you weren't when I tackled him about it.'

'Yes, well ...' Jeff sighed and flexed a wide shoulder. 'There was no need for you to do that. Them's the breaks, I guess, and it's all water under the bridge now, anyway. Now how about some of those rings you're holding, hmm?'

'You're going to take the prizes you won yesterday?' she countered, accepting his decision to change the subject gratefully as she separated the requisite number but refrained from actually passing them to him.

'Okay, okay.' He gave in after a few moments on seeing the adamant look on her face. 'Provided they're all boxes of chocolates,' he added a late condition.

In order that he could distribute them among his family's female guests, Taryn surmised. After all, they were a good brand of confectionary and a nice selection. 'All right,' she assented, now condescending to accept his money in return for the rings she was holding. 'Although you are entitled to a watch if you want it, you know.'

'Mmm, but how many watches can you wear?' he grinned with a significant look at the expensive model already encircling his wrist before he took aim. 'Besides, I know who I can give the chocolates to.'

Just as she had surmised, thought Taryn, and watched wryly as he calmly won another two boxes from her. Selecting the six prettily patterned boxes from the shelves behind her, she placed them in a pile on the counter.

'There!' she exclaimed on a satisfied note. 'They're all yours.'

'Meaning, your conscience is now clear, is that it?' Jeff smiled and, after receiving her endorsing nod, picked them up, but only to immediately put them down again right in front of her. 'Then I present them all to you as a gift. And don't say I can't,' accurately anticipating her reaction, 'because I very definitely can. As you said, I won them, so they're mine to give to whoever I please, and it pleases me to give them to you. Not only in thanks for your very pleasant company last night, but also as a parting gift because I doubt there'll be an opportunity for us to get together again before you leave, what with you having to pack all your equipment up, and me helping to see all our guests get away all right.'

'But I imagined they were for . . .' she started, and then stopped with a helpless laugh. 'You're tricky, Jeff Douglas, you know that, don't you? But thank you all the same. It was a nice gesture.' A slight pause, and, 'However, as much as I'll be sorry to see you go, I think it's time you were leaving, or else you're likely to have Slade searching you out again.' As he had on more than that one occasion the evening before, she recollected. 'So I'll just say goodbye and hope circumstances allow us to meet again next year.'

'I'll look forward to it,' he smiled and, bending closer, pulled her towards him with a hand around the back of her neck in order to drop a friendly kiss on to her smooth forehead. 'I also hope things pick up for you in Linwood.'

'Thanks,' she acknowledged appreciatively, knowing he wasn't merely being polite but really meant it. 'And I hope your brother doesn't continue giving you a hard time because it was his money you lost.'

'Since he's already been repaid, there's no fear of that,' he advised negligently, to her relief, and lifting a hand in a sketchy salute he began moving away.

Taryn watched him depart with a fond smile. She'd liked Jeff. Not in any romantic sense, but just as a companion who had proved to be a very enjoyable and likeable escort, and she was a little sorry that it would be at least a year, if not longer, before there would be any likelihood of her seeing him again.

As the evening progressed, with no noticeable

increase in custom at the sideshows, Taryn's father began dismantling his stall before the show was actually over and, taking her cue from him, Taryn started to do likewise. As both her father and herself were working alone, she supposed her brother to have been helping their mother do the same with her stall, but it wasn't until Luke made a surprise and somewhat secretive appearance in the darkness behind her cubicle that she realised that wasn't what he had been doing at all.

'Hey! Get a load of this.' His first low, but evidently excited call had her moving into the shadowed area curiously. A curiosity that abruptly turned to incredulity on seeing the over-full leather wallet he was holding out for her inspection.

'Where on earth did you find it?' she quizzed in an amazed tone. 'There must be a fortune in there.'

'Not quite, but I reckon it's close to a thousand. I haven't had a chance to count it yet,' Luke advised in a rather breathless voice that suggested he may have been running, and in consequence had a little wariness creeping in with Taryn's astonishment. 'As to where I found it . . .' He gave a half shrug, his mouth curving with obvious gratification. 'Well, if you really want to know, it was in that arrogant Slade Douglas's hip pocket.'

'It was *where*?' his sister's horrified disbelief had her exclaiming on a rising note.

'Sssh! Keep your voice down! Do you want everyone to know about it?' he retorted fiercely. 'I said, to put it bluntly, that I lifted it from Slade Douglas! It serves him right for carrying so much with him.'

Taryn felt as if she was taking part in a bad dream. 'For God's sake, Luke, that's just plain stealing! And how much is in there has nothing to do with it! You've got to give it back! Say you found it, or something, but just give it back, please!'

'No way!' he refused her entreaty promptly, his tone turning huffy. 'Not that he'd be likely to believe I found it, anyway, but why the hell should I? I'm not having him accusing *my* sister of cheating his stinking family, and I figured this was the most apt method to get our revenge ... through the hip pocket!' He uttered a short, mocking laugh. 'It seemed to hit a nerve there yesterday when his brother got rolled, and it's the only way the likes of you and me have to effectively retaliate against his kind.'

Revenge—rolled—retaliate! Taryn could hardly credit what he was saying. 'So who said we wanted to retaliate? I certainly didn't! And I thought you said that game was honest yesterday. You don't get *rolled* when it's on the level, Luke!'

'An erroneous choice of words,' he claimed sulkily, but the fact that he wouldn't, or couldn't, look her in the eye as he said it gave rise to the deepest misgivings, and disappointment, on his sister's part. 'In any case, the money will come in handy for that set of tyres Dad ...'

'Are you mad?' she broke in on him, aghast. 'Dad will skin you alive if he discovers what you've done!' Hesitating, she put out a pleading hand. 'Oh, please, Luke, just return it, will you? There's going to be hell to pay if you don't.'

'Not if you keep your mouth shut about where it came from!'

'And by so doing become an accessory? No, thanks! Our family has managed to get by without resorting to such means until now and I, for one, intend to continue in the same fashion ... as I've no doubt you would be too if it wasn't for that shifty Sam Cowper! He's evidently not a good influence on you, Luke, and it's becoming equally plain that you'd be a lot better off if you weren't in his company so often.'

Luke lifted his head defiantly. 'Sam's all right! You just don't like him because he's down to earth and doesn't put on the dog.'

An understatement if ever she had heard one, grimaced Taryn. Sam was quite the most unrefined character it had ever been her misfortune to meet, and he certainly didn't pretend to be anything he wasn't!

'In any event,' she suddenly realised her brother was continuing, 'it's not a matter of you becoming an accessory where Mum and Dad are concerned. It's more a case of what they don't know won't hurt them. Provided you don't tell them differently, they'll just think I won a bit more than usual at cards, nothing else.'

'But you still stole it, Luke!' she tried to impress on him urgently, a hint of anger entering her voice now as her initial feelings of shock started to wear off. Good grief, couldn't he see that, no matter even if he did plan to help their parents with the money, the ends didn't justify the means? 'And if you won't return it, then I will!' She made to snatch the wallet out of his hand.

Unluckily, from Taryn's point of view, he must have sensed what she intended when she first began, for his reflexes in whipping it out of her reach were just too fast for her. 'Oh, no, you don't!' he half laughed, his success in thwarting her intention undoubtedly the reason for his lightening mood. 'It's mine and I aim to . . .' All of a sudden he came to an abrupt halt, his whole demeanour altering as he stared past her along the concourse. A hasty look over her own shoulder explaining to his sister just why he should appear so markedly nervous now as she also caught sight of Slade, his expression nothing short of thunderous, purposefully striding in their direction. 'I don't believe it! He couldn't possibly know who ... Well, whether he does or not, I'm not taking any chances. Listen ...!' Luke now urged in an agitated voice as he shrank further back into the shadows. 'I'm off! Thank God, I left the bike behind Dad's gallery! But if Douglas does say anything to you, just cover for me, okay?' Turning, he started hurrying away, then stopped before disappearing around the next stall. 'Oh, and tell Mum and Dad that I'll meet up with them along the road somewhere. If not before Linwood, then after.' Following which instruction he spun round once more and started running.

A minute or so later Taryn heard the throaty roar of his motorbike as it flared into powerful life, saw him momentarily as he set off across the back of the showground at a furious pace and, stunned by the suddenness with which it had all occurred, presently found herself facing an obviously infuriated Slade with her thoughts in turmoil.

His evidently weren't suffering from any such confusion, though, because immediately on reaching her he grabbed hold of her arm in a punishing grip and demanded on a grating note, 'All right, where's he gone?'

Taryn could only lick at her lips shakily, too flustered to even think of attempting to free herself. 'Wh-who?' she stammered, her brother's plea for her to cover for him coming to mind unbidden.

'Your long-haired, light-fingered lout of a brother, naturally! The one who just took off from here in a panic, like the lily-livered coward his thieving type usually is? And with my wallet still grasped in his sweaty hand, no doubt!' he elucidated savagely. 'Or did he leave it with you—his partner—for safe keeping?' He shook her roughly.

Taryn's foremost feeling was one of plummeting despair. So he knew who had taken his wallet! She had been desperately hoping that his presence had somehow been connected with the events of yesterday. Still, she felt obligated to continue protecting her younger brother as best she could.

'No, he didn't give me anything for safe keeping, and neither am I his partner as you keep inferring!' she denied with a trace of resentment as her thoughts became more composed at last. 'And—and what makes you think he has your wallet, anyhow? If you've lost it, maybe you dropped it. Why automatically suspect Luke?'

The fingers around her arm tightened their grip painfully. 'Because he was seen relieving me of it, that's why!' he ground out, harshly mocking. 'And I notice you don't appear surprised by the information.'

Despondent, yes, but surprised . . .? How could she evince such an emotion after hearing the truth from her brother's own lips? 'Pr-probably because I'm becoming used to you making s-such accusations about my family,' she evaded, albeit rather jerkily. 'And I'd be pleased if you'd let go of my arm,' making an effort to drag herself away now. 'I don't know what you think gives you the right to assault me in such a fashion . . .'

'Oh, don't try playing the persecuted innocent with me, honey!' he broke in on her scornfully. 'It's been apparent ever since yesterday that you're involved in his fraudulent schemes right up to your neck!'

'That's not true!' Taryn burst out indignantly,

wishing her father would come to her rescue, even
though since shortly after Luke's arrival she hadn't
seen hide nor hair of him. 'My brother and I go our
own separate ways, and I have nothing whatsoever to
do with his gambling, or—or anything else!'

'Yeah, yeah ... sure!' Slade's voice was totally,
derisively unbelieving. 'That's why you were the first
person he ran to with his ill-gotten gains, I suppose.'

'So why shouldn't he come to see me whenever he
chooses? We are closely related, when all's said and
done!' Her eyes widened facetiously. 'But that doesn't
make me his keeper ... or his partner!'

'Although, since you were the last person to speak to
him before he departed in such a guilty rush, you *do*
know where he's gone,' he returned to his initial
question stonily, insistently.

'No, I do not,' she refuted in equally clipped tones.
'And even if I did, I wouldn't tell you. I've only your
word for it that someone did see Luke take your
wallet. For all I know, you could have made that up
just to lend weight to your unfair determination to
blame my brother whenever one of your family
happens to lose some money.'

'With good reason, I'd say!' The curve of his mouth
became caustically pronounced. 'But if you don't want
to co-operate—I had thought to settle the matter
without involving the police—then by all means let's
collect my witness and we'll all go down town and see
what conclusions the local sergeant comes up with.'
He paused. 'It may even be worthwhile to ask him to
check with other towns you've been through. The
results of such enquiries could prove very interesting,
I'm sure, considering how practised your brother and
his—er—other working partner appeared to be
yesterday.'

His last threat had Taryn drawing in a shuddering breath. Oh, God, if such a check was made, despite those previous investigations having come to nought, it could still be sufficient to cause another one to be held in Jinda Jinda, which added to the fact that Luke had, by his own admission, deliberately stolen Slade's wallet, and in the presence of a witness too apparently, would mean nothing could save him from the consequences of his actions this time.

On the heels of her alarm, a brief spurt of anger surged through Taryn at having been left to face the music on her brother's behalf, especially when she had been the one to urge him to return the wallet, as well as in protest at Slade's unfounded claims that she was in league with Luke. And because the man holding her was the only one present of the two, it was he who received her irate glare.

'The local sergeant also being one of your family, I presume, if you're in a position to dictate to him what course he should follow!' she sniped. 'And that being so, then naturally he'll take your word—no matter how fanciful—against that of a stranger who's simply passing through, won't he? From what I've been told the place should evidently be called Douglastown, not Jinda Jinda!'

'Quite possibly,' Slade conceded, the dipping angle of his dark head provoking in the extreme. 'However, I can assure you Harvey Summerville, our resident reprensetative of the law, has absolutely no connection with any family in town, Douglas or otherwise, because he was only transferred here from Melbourne five years ago. So shall we go?' Both his tone and his grip hardened as he made to force her into accompanying him.

'No! You're not dragging me along with you like

some criminal on parade, particularly when I haven't done anything!' she fumed, struggling to break away from him more frantically now.

'Okay,' he took her completely by surprise by suddenly agreeing, and finally consenting to turn her loose. 'I guess it's not possible, even for a family like yours, to all do a moonlight flit on such notice. Not if it means having to leave all this equipment behind, at any rate. Or do you simply acquire equipment as you need it . . . in the same way you do ready cash?' His well-shaped brows rose to a sarcastic peak.

'Oh, you arrogant swine!' Taryn almost choked in her fury, swinging a hand towards his face with all the force she could gather. 'Don't you dare include my parents in your odious accusations! Don't you dare!'

Captured in mid-flight by a hand that blatantly displayed its greater strength, her wrist was now used as a means to haul her within inches of a tautly held, powerfully muscular form. 'And don't *you* dare lift your hand to me again, or it may be more than just your wrist that suffers next time!' he threatened with one last emphasising squeeze before releasing her disdainfully.

'Then leave my parents out of it—they know nothing about any of this—or it may be more than just my hand that I lift against *you* next time!' she had a warning of her own to impart in return. Not even if he had broken her wrist could she have allowed him to get away with insinuating her parents were in any way involved too.

For a second or two Slade watched her silently, his dark grey eyes appearing nearly black in the dim light, their expression unreadable in consequence. 'Is that so?' he eventually remarked, sounding distinctly unimpressed. 'Then how is it that you don't defend your brother with the same vehemence, I wonder? Because you know as well as I do that he's as guilty as it's possible to be?' When she didn't immediately answer, he shrugged. 'Well, no matter, I doubt the police will have any trouble in getting to the truth of it.'

Taryn caught at her lip anxiously with shining white teeth. 'You still mean to see them, then?'

'Of course!' His affirmation came with a ruthless decisiveness. 'Right now, as a matter of fact. While there's still a chance for them to pick your brother up on the road somewhere.'

'Oh, but you can't! Don't ... please!' she forced herself to implore as he made to leave. She couldn't just stand by and watch while her brother was sent to jail, in spite of hating having to ask anything of this man.

'Why not?' he countered without any sign of a weakening in his resolve, although he had at least halted, she noted. 'Because as I said, you know damn well he's guilty?'

Swallowing convulsively, she finally gave a dejected nod. 'But he's not really bad, just young and a little weak at times, that's all,' she valiantly attempted to convince him. 'And—and at the moment he's in with a man who—who's not really a good influence on him, I don't think.'

'His working partner?' he hazarded.

Taryn nodded again.

'So what do you expect me to do about it? Forget the whole matter just because you've been compelled to tell the truth at last? That's all the more reason for me to carry out my intention of seeing the police, wouldn't you say?'

She shook her head anguishedly in response to both

his question and the sound of unsparing determination in his voice. 'I ... *I'll* pay you back, then,' she suddenly offered, her amethyst-coloured eyes lifting to his hopefully. 'That way there won't be any necessity for you to go to the police. I mean, it's getting back the money you lost that's important, isn't it?'

'So he did pass my wallet on to you after all, you bloody little liar!'

'No!' Taryn hurled her denial back at him resentfully. 'I've already told you I don't have it! I was meaning I would repay you out of my own money!'

He arched a sardonic brow. 'From what Jeff's had to say regarding how slow business has been for you, I wouldn't have thought you had a spare fifteen hundred laying around.'

Taryn gulped. 'There was *that* much in the wallet?' It appeared Luke had been considerably wide of the mark in his calculation!

'Uh-huh,' he confirmed in a drawl. 'Normally I don't carry such an amount with me, but it happens that I sold a couple of young dogs today and was paid in cash.'

'I see. Well ...' She shifted awkwardly beneath his unwavering grey gaze. 'What Jeff told you was correct. We haven't been doing too well this year, in particular. People just don't seem to be spending as much on sideshows these days. Not like they used to.'

One corner of his mouth sloped cynically. 'If that's an attempt to play on my sympathies, honey, then don't bother! Where you and your brother are concerned, I just don't have any! So let's just get down to the nitty-gritty, huh? Have you got the money to repay it, or haven't you?'

'I—well—not in a lump sum, exactly,' she murmured uncomfortably.

'Meaning?' His eyes narrowed suspiciously.

She took a deep breath. 'I was thinking of sending it to you in—in instalments, actually,' she revealed in a rush.

Slade laughed, disparagingly. 'Oh, no, I'm not falling for that one! And if that's the best you can offer, then it's obvious I'm wasting my time!' Once again he turned, preparing to leave.

Taryn cast about frantically for some other solution, and came up with, 'I—I'll put myself up as security, then!'

Halting, he swung back to face her with a frown. 'And just what do you mean by that?'

'I'll stay in town and get a job until the money's repaid,' she explained breathlessly.

'In instalments?' he mocked.

The satirical derision in his tone nettled, and irate sparks flashed in her dark fringed, violet-blue eyes. 'There's not much else I can do! At least I have offered to repay it!'

Unperturbed by her show of anger, he merely shrugged. 'So just who's going to give you this job? They're not exactly two a penny nowadays, especially in a town the size of Jinda Jinda.'

'I'll still find one somehow!' she vowed with more confidence than she actually felt. Unfortunately, he was right in what he said.

'Then promptly leave town the moment I'm out of sight,' he charged on a jeering note. 'Honey, I wouldn't trust you as far as I could throw you!'

'No, I wouldn't leave town! I've given my word that I'll repay what's owed to you, and I meant it!' she defended hotly. Then, on the spur of the moment as an idea occurred, she eyed him speculatively from beneath the shadow of her long lashes. 'However, if you're so untrusting, why not keep me in sight, then? *You* employ me!'

'Me?' For once she seemed to have taken him by surprise as he stared back at her, askance. But not for long, though, she noted disappointedly. 'And why should I do that? A man who invites a fox—sorry, vixen—into his hen-house is only asking for trouble,' he proposed drily.

'By that, I take it you're implying I'm likely to knock off the family silver, or something similar, if given half a chance!' Taryn smouldered. 'God! What does it take to convince you that I wasn't included in Luke's activities?' She raked a hand through her red-gold hair distractedly, glints of fire making an appearance where it caught the light.

'A damn sight more than what I've seen to date, I can tell you that!' He let his thoughts be known in no uncertain terms. 'Besides . . .' he continued in a more moderate tone, an unexpected touch of wry humour evident even, 'you expect me to employ you so you can repay me with my own money?'

She hadn't thought of it in that way, but now that he'd mentioned it, she supposed it was too much to expect. 'It was only a thought,' she sighed, her own anger subsiding beneath the weight of despondency that was again descending upon her. 'I was simply trying to find some way to prove to you that I was perfectly serious about wanting to repay the money.'

'Hmm . . .' Crossing his arms across his broad chest, Slade gazed down at her in silent contemplation momentarily, and then his firmly moulded mouth surprisingly began to curve into a smile. But a somewhat whimsical smile that Taryn just couldn't find an adequate reason for and, as a result, had a certain wariness entering her eyes. 'Maybe the idea does have some merit, after all,' he mused. 'My mother's been saying for some time now that she needs help with all her committee work, and the dogs, or rather the pups we have at the moment, have been taking up a lot of my time of late that could perhaps have been put to better use elsewhere.' His head tilted quizzically. 'Have you ever had any experience in working with animals?'

'Only the two-legged kind,' she quipped with a grimace, but trying not to let him see that she included him in that category.

None the less, from the slight narrowing of his gaze she suspected he may not have required any help from her to deduce that, and she averted her face swiftly, unconsciously holding her breath as she waited for his anticipated, and undoubtedly biting comment. When it didn't come, she chanced a hesitant look upwards again and found that was exactly what he'd been waiting for as her eyes promptly connected with a pair of shrewd grey ones.

'A word of advice, honey,' he began in a deceptively lazy drawl. 'If you're having second thoughts already, then I suggest you come right out and say so, because I'll be getting my money back one way or the other, believe me! So if you want out . . .' He spread one hand in an indifferent gesture.

'No, no, of course I don't!' she demurred swiftly. Although she was beginning to have some reservations at the thought of working for someone who didn't bother to conceal his low opinion of her, and who was as hard as iron into the bargain! 'I simply meant—I was only . . .' Deciding she was more than likely to only make it worse if she continued, she lapsed into a discomforted, but protective silence.

'Wise girl,' he applauded in a provoking tone that

took all the willpower Taryn possessed to avoid telling *him* exactly what she thought of him. 'So what about your parents? Won't they have something to say about your leaving them in the lurch, as it were?'

'They'll be surprised, naturally,' she owned in tightly controlled accents. And no wonder, on such short notice! 'Although I can't imagine them trying to stop me. It will mean extra work for them while I'm away, of course, but they used to manage more or less on their own when Luke and I were younger, and with business not so hectic these days, hopefully it won't be all that difficult for them.'

'They won't consider it strange you being the one to stay behind in order to pay off their son's debts?' His brows arched expressively. 'Or has it come to this before?'

'No! Because whether you believe it or not, this is the very first time anything like this has ever happened!' she flared. 'In any case, I don't intend telling them the real reason for my wanting to remain behind. It would be too upsetting for my mother, while as for Dad . . .' She exhaled eloquently. 'Well, there's no telling what he might do. Really give Luke what-for, most probably!'

'Sounds just what he needs!' succinctly.

In view of just what she was being forced to do in order to save her brother's neck, Taryn was inclined to agree with him, although loyalty dictated that she didn't admit as much aloud, and particularly to the man with her.

'So what reason will you give them?' Slade now enquired.

She shook her head indecisively. 'I'm not sure yet. I should be able to think of something, though, that will satisfy them.'

'Mmm, I'm sure you will,' he averred with a sardonic inflection she took to mean that lying was second nature to her. 'And will they also accept your brother's sudden departure just as unquestioningly?'

'More than likely if I tell them that he simply decided to take off again for a couple of days,' she shrugged. 'He's done it before when . . .'

'Things have been getting too hot for him?' he interposed sardonically.

'No! When he feels like a change of scene from shows,' she corrected sharply. Pausing, she rubbed the palms of her hands down the sides of her jeans nervously. She had a question of her own to ask, but was both reluctant to voice it, and to hear his answer. 'And—and will you be telling Jeff and your mother the true reason you're employing me?'

'Don't you think I should?'

So he did mean to. She should have known! Involuntarily, her soft lower lip began to tremble and she half turned away, her head drooping disconsolately. 'That's up to you, I guess,' she just managed to push out in a shaky whisper.

Beside her, Slade expelled a slow, heavy breath, and then an ensnaring hand beneath her chin was abruptly tilting her troubled face upwards again. 'Not necessarily on this occasion,' he asserted quietly.

A frown flickered across her smooth forehead. 'I don't understand.'

'There was a witness, remember? And although I didn't say anything about it before coming down here, Phil may have done so in my absence.'

'I see,' she sighed dismally. Followed almost immediately by an apprehensive, 'He wouldn't also have told the police, would he?'

He gave a brief shake of his head. 'I shouldn't think

so. I told him to leave it to me—that I'd handle it. There wasn't any reason for him to take the matter further.'

Taryn sighed again—this time with thankfulness—but unaccountably becoming aware of his touch in a physical sense all of a sudden, dropped her gaze in confusion and pulled away from him agitatedly. 'Well, at least that's something, I suppose,' she murmured, trying to make the best of it, as well as regain her composure. 'So when does my period of employment begin?'

Slade's shapely mouth took on a wry slant. 'Anxious to get started, hmm?'

'Anxious to have it end as soon as possible, you mean!' she corrected, recovered now from her temporary loss of countenance.

'In that case, in the morning, I guess. I'll be heading back to the property at about eight. Can you be ready by then?'

'I'll be ready,' she affirmed with an emphasising nod. 'Where shall I meet you?'

'At the office in the back of the Members' Stand. I want to pick up some papers from there before I leave.'

Taryn nodded her compliance. Then, because he had made it so plain that he was still suspicious of her, couldn't resist gibing lightly, 'You're sure you can trust me to still be here by then?'

'Uh-huh . . . I reckon,' he drawled, lazily confident. 'Not only because you know what the result of such an action would mean with regard to your brother, but also because we're only camped over there ourselves.' Indicating a group of luxurious caravans and a large marquee that occupied a secluded site just outside the showground's wire boundary fence. 'Which means, of course, that it would be almost impossible for you to make an unscheduled departure without my being aware of it.'

'So it would,' she grimaced tartly, wondering why she hadn't associated the exclusive set-up which had caught her attention previously with him before. It had been patently clear that the Douglases had been staying in Jinda Jinda, and with thirty guests or so to accommodate, where better to do so than in such select and comfortable surroundings? 'You've got it all worked out, haven't you?'

'I figured it would be advisable,' he owned in the most mocking manner he had yet used as, with a slight incline of his head, he began moving away.

This time Taryn didn't stop him, but with a last scowl at his broad back, returned her attention to what she had been doing before Luke had so disastrously interrupted her. Without Slade's constraining and menacing presence, she was now able to view the circumstances she found herself in a little more fully, and certainly a whole lot more leisurely.

Whether this was a benefit or not she couldn't quite decide, because the more she went over it in her mind the more she began to speculate whether she should simply have shut her mouth and allowed Luke to take his own medicine. It wasn't that she regretted trying to shield him, but rather it was because she was starting to feel nervously in need of some protection herself! On first seeing Slade she had predicted he would make a daunting foe, and she wasn't relishing one little bit the thought of having that relentlessness directed solely at herself!

CHAPTER THREE

THE next morning Taryn's parents wanted to remain with her at the showgrounds until she met Slade, but as she was fearful of what he might say to them she was relieved when she was finally able to persuade them it wasn't necessary and for them to leave at seven, as they normally did when making for a new town. With their departure, however, came the feeling of having burnt her bridges behind her and, lighting a calming cigarette, she took a seat on the wooden bench outside the Members' Stand office and prepared to wait out the next hour as unworriedly as possible.

In actual fact, there was one aspect of her impending employment she was quite looking forward to. The notion of staying in one place for more than just a couple of days. It was something she had often secretly yearned for while she was on the road—as much to see if it did hold the attraction she believed it to, or if it bored her after a time. Of course, whether she found it to her liking would depend to a large extent upon just how agreeably, or otherwise, her time spent with the Douglases turned out to be, she mused contemplatively, but right at the moment not even that knowledge could entirely quell her feelings of subdued eagerness.

Slade arrived at ten to eight, dressed in dark brown moleskins and a sheepskin jacket in deference to the decidedly cool wind that was successfully keeping the temperature down.

'I'm sorry to have kept you waiting, but there were

things I had to attend to at the camp,' he advised cursorily as he unlocked the office door.

'That's all right,' Taryn shrugged, surprised a little by his unexpected apology. 'It's not eight yet, anyway.'

About to step inside, he fixed her with a chaffing look. 'Mmm, but you forget, from the camp I could see what time you got here.'

'Oh!' She coloured irritably. So he had been spying on her without her knowledge, had he? No doubt in order to ensure she couldn't break her word!

'Meanwhile, you can wait in the car, if you like,' he went on in a return to his original perfunctory tone, nodding towards the white station wagon he had arrived in. 'I shouldn't be long in here, but it will probably be warmer for you out of the wind.'

Appreciating the unanticipated consideration—it had been cold on the seat—Taryn injected a similar crispness into her own voice as she clipped out a grateful acknowledgment. They were employer and employee now, and she supposed Slade would expect her to cultivate a suitably businesslike manner too.

Picking up her single suitcase, she made her way over to the vehicle and opening the rear door, lifted her case into the back. Deducing that although they weren't with him now, his mother and Jeff would most likely be travelling with them as well, she then slid on to the bluey-grey, plushly upholstered seat inside.

Presently, Slade reappeared with a bulging folder in his hand, and after re-locking the office walked briskly to the station wagon and seated himself behind the wheel. In a continuation of the same economic movement he then half turned in order to toss the folder on to the back seat beside Taryn, his glance turning sardonic as it came to rest on her.

'I'm not your chauffeur, honey, so why don't you just move into the front, huh?' he drawled.

Feeling unbelievably nervous now that their actual moment of departure was at hand, Taryn scrambled self-consciously to do as he suggested. 'I—I'm sorry, I didn't mean to imply that you were,' she stammered as soon as she had re-seated herself next to him. 'I merely thought to leave room for your mother and Jeff.'

'Except that they returned to the property late last night,' wryly. Leaning forward to switch on the ignition, he soon had them moving off smoothly. 'Also, I could have put that case in there for you.' Nodding towards the back. 'There was no need for you to have done it.'

She raised a deprecating shoulder. 'It wasn't heavy, and I didn't want it to look as if I expected you to do it for me. After all, you are my employer now, Mr Douglas.'

'Mr Douglas?' He flicked her a satirically askance glance. 'My, we are formal this morning, aren't we?' A slight pause. 'Or are you simply attempting to disarm me with all this uncustomary submissiveness?'

'No!' she disclaimed with a gulp, aghast that he should have misconstrued her intentions to such a degree. 'I—I merely thought you would want me to adopt a businesslike approach, and—and under the circumstances I wasn't sure just what I should call you.'

'How about . . . Slade?' he proposed drily. 'Seeing that's my name, it would seem appropriate, don't you think?'

Taryn flushed at the inherent mockery in his voice. 'I s-suppose so,' she allowed miserably. Even when she was trying to do the right thing, he couldn't wait to find fault! At the same time, though, and because he had seen fit to first decry and then taunt her for her efforts, she now felt entitled to point out with a touch of reproof, 'While my name is Taryn . . . not honey!'

'I'll try to remember,' he drawled, the captivatingly humorous quirk to his mouth making an abrupt and unexpected appearance which promptly had her suspecting he wouldn't be making any such endeavour at all unless it suited him, even as it had her pulse racing erratically, unpredictably, in response.

Looking away quickly, she tried concentrating on the passing countryside, hoping to dismiss him from her thoughts completely, but it appeared not even the profusion of spring flowers that were coming in to bloom everywhere were capable of doing that, for her thoughts remained waywardly fixed on her companion.

What she really couldn't understand was why he had affected her in such a fashion in the first place. Oh, he was certainly good-looking enough—that was about the very first thing she had noticed about him, after all—and his attitude towards herself this morning had definitely been less disparaging than usual, but surely she wasn't so adolescent that that, together with the beginnings of a half smile, was all it took to have her going weak at the knees? She decided it was more likely to be simply a symptom of her continuing tenseness due to the circumstances surrounding her employment and resolutely made herself turn to face him again.

'How much further is it to—to . . . the property?'

she asked determinedly, if a little hesitantly. 'Jeff did mention the name, but I seem to have forgotten.'

'Merringannee Bluff,' he supplied impassively. 'And it's about another thirty-five miles.' He sent her a rather cynical look. 'Why? Were you hoping it would be closer to town?'

Sensing another of his criticisms—and that just when she had believed his attitude had improved?—Taryn did her best to keep her annoyance from showing. 'Not at all,' she denied in as level a tone as possible. 'I was merely interested to know how far we had to travel.' She paused, her resentment getting the better of her as she widened her eyes sarcastically. 'I didn't realise it was supposed to be a secret!'

Slade didn't answer. He flicked her a darkening grey gaze instead that had her subsiding into a protective, but still indignant, silence again, which this time lasted for several miles.

'By the way . . .' It was Slade who eventually ended the quiet, and on an unusually deep note. 'I'm sorry, but I've some disappointing news for you . . .'

'Oh?' Taryn's stomach muscles tightened convulsively, and suddenly recalling something from the night before, questioned fearfully, 'That—that man who saw Luke . . . he didn't go to the police, after all, did he?'

He shook his head reassuringly. 'No, Phil didn't go to the police, but unfortunately, by the time I returned, he had told my mother and Jeff just what had occurred.'

'I see,' she nodded abjectly as a shudder of despair went through her. 'S-so they—kn-know . . .' Her voice shook so much that she had to stop and take a couple of deep breaths before trying again. 'So they know now why I'm working for you too.'

'No, as a matter of fact they don't.' His surprising contradiction had her eyeing him perplexedly. 'Actually, I told them I'd managed to recover my wallet from your brother, and that my employing you was a separate matter entirely.'

'Oh, thank you,' she breathed fervently, though hardly able to credit he would deceive anyone, let alone members of his own family, on her behalf. Not when she knew he regarded her as only slightly less conniving than Luke! 'That was very ... considerate of you.'

'Noble too, considering what my dear mother had to say on the matter, anyway,' Slade suddenly laughed wryly, expressively.

Never having seen him really laugh before, Taryn now found herself liking it too much for her own good. 'She doesn't agree with you employing me, I gather,' she deduced, compelling herself to pursue the conversation in an effort to ignore his stirring image.

He half inclined his head in a rueful gesture. 'Mother's a stickler for respectability and, by virtue of your close connection to Luke, I'm afraid that in her estimation, that tends to make you somewhat unacceptable also, honey.'

'To you too most times, apparently.' The sighed half gibe came almost of its own volition, although without any accompanying protest at his continuing use of a nickname. At the moment she had more important matters to worry about.

'With good reason in my case, I would have said.' His return was promptly, meaningfully voiced, and suspecting she would only be wasting her breath in attempting to refute his misconception again, Taryn exhaled defeatedly.

'And—and is that how Jeff feels about it as well?' was her next tentative query.

A sardonic twist caught at his lips. 'No, you've somehow managed to convince him you're entirely innocent. He's merely surprised, though none the less delighted,' with a mocking nuance, 'that you've decided to stay around here for the time being. Particularly in view of your having said nothing to him about any such plan.'

'So what reason did you give for my doing so? And for your agreeing to employ me at all, if it comes to that?' she now asked curiously, and a little more brightly. At least it was something to know that Jeff believed in her. If he hadn't, she·didn't know what she would have done. As it was, it didn't augur very well for an especially pleasant period of employment considering the opinions held by the other two members of his family.

Slade shrugged negligently, not taking his eyes from the road. 'I simply said that, on the spur of the moment, you'd happened to express a wish to remain in the area a little longer and had asked me if I knew of anyone hereabouts who had an employment vacancy. Whereupon, and equally impulsively,' with his mouth shaping wryly, 'I mentioned that as a matter of fact I'd been contemplating hiring someone, as a result of which you asked if you might be that someone, and I agreed because I considered you were entitled to a chance to prove you weren't involved in your brother's schemes.'

Taryn digested the information thoughtfully. It was a pity then that he didn't actually believe that instead of just pretending to! she grimaced. As he could have if he'd only listened with an open mind when she had originally denied having been included in Luke's activities rather than having already jumped to the wrong conclusion!

'So tell me, what story did you come up with for your parents' edification on the matter?' Slade suddenly interrupted her reverie to enquire.

'Oh—er—something not so altogether different,' she faltered, trying to dismiss her previous reproachful thoughts. After all, she supposed she should just be thankful that he hadn't disclosed the truth! 'I just told them that, as I'd been toying with the idea of settling down in one place for a while now—which they knew to be true because I had mentioned something of the kind to them before—and in order to see if I liked it as much as anything, I thought here seemed as good a place as any to try, especially since I already knew Jeff and it was his brother who had offered me employment while I decided.'

'Offered?' He turned to look at her with one dark brow peaking expressively.

'Well, I could hardly tell them the truth, and—and it seemed less likely to cause any awkward comments than anything else I could have said! Besides, that was certainly no worse a white lie than yours to the effect that you felt I was entitled to a chance to prove my innocence!' she fired back in defence.

His grey eyes filled with a goading light. 'Except that mine was done solely on someone else's behalf, while yours was entirely on your own!'

'Something you undoubtedly don't intend to either forgive, or allow me to forget, I'm sure!' she retaliated on a sniping note even as a touch of pink invaded her honey tinted cheeks on recognising the accuracy of his contention.

'And since it was only due to your pleading, out of fear for what might befall your brother otherwise, that

I relented and agreed to employ you, is there any reason why I shouldn't?'

'Yes!' she had no hesitation in stating as a sudden remembrance flashed into her mind. 'Because if it hadn't suited you as well in some way, then I'm positive nothing I could have said would have made you accept me as your employee.'

'Suited me . . . how?' he half laughed as if amused by the suggestion.

'I—I don't know exactly,' she was forced into admitting, reluctantly, since it was only a suspicion brought on by a certain unexplainable look on his face at the time. 'But I figure it must have somehow, otherwise why agree to the idea at all?' She sent him a somewhat triumphant look.

The one she received in return was distinctly mocking. 'Maybe, because you pleaded so heart-rendingly,' he drawled. 'And just maybe, because *I* figured it was probably the quickest method of having my money repaid.' Pausing, his expression became even more taunting. 'Or have you forgotten that I'm still out the small amount of some fifteen hundred dollars?'

'How could I?' she immediately countered in caustic tones. 'That's the only reason I'm subjecting myself to your—your . . .' on the verge of saying, insufferable authority, she prudently altered it to, 'hiring of me.'

If Slade noticed the slight hesitation, he didn't show it as he shot back, 'Good! And now you know the reason for my having agreed to it, don't you?'

Did she? For some unknown reason Taryn still wasn't wholly convinced. Okay, so he wanted his money repaid, but at the same time she was sure there had been something else that had occasioned his agreement. Meanwhile, however, he was evidently expecting an answer and she hunched her shoulder nearest to him in a simulated gesture of deprecation.

'If you say so,' she allowed, sweetly acquiescent. 'I mean, when all's said and done, you're the boss ... boss.'

'You'd better believe it!'

The less than encouraging retort had her heaving a rather disgruntled sigh and looking out of the window once more. Perhaps she shouldn't have made such a quip, she granted, but did he really have to be quite so explicitly squashing? From the way he acted, anyone would think she was the one who had taken his money, not the one who had *volunteered* to repay it!

And when they did reach the property there was going to be his parent to contend with too, she recalled with an involuntary shiver, all her prior nervousness returning in full force. A parent, moreover, who wasn't only averse to her having been employed, but one who—judging by Jeff and Slade's remarks on the night of the dance—was very conscious of her position in society as well as apparently being something of a matriarchal martinet also! Oh, she could just see the months ahead were going to be pure purgatory! she predicted ruefully.

One thing her disheartening musings did prompt Taryn to wonder, though, was just how Slade, in particular, and his mother got along together. With a surreptitious gaze from beneath her dusky lashes she studied the strong profile presented to her, noting again the self-assured angle at which he held his dark head, the firm, attractive mouth, and the bold and determined set of his jaw. No, she decided, he wasn't a man to meekly do anyone's bidding, let alone a woman's, even if that woman did happen to be his mother.

By which token, she went on to reason, it would
have to follow that Slade was the final authority at
Merringannee Bluff and not his parent, and strangely
she found the thought slightly reassuring, although
she couldn't have said why with any degree of
certainty. Probably it was purely a case of 'better the
devil you know, than the one you don't', came the
rueful surmise, but it did at least enable her to
complete the journey in a rather less anxious state of
mind.

In due course their approach to the homestead was
made after turning off the road and crossing a wide
stock grid, then proceeding for another mile or so over
comparatively flat land, the hard, sandy track they
were now following bordered by yellow gums, sheoaks
and pepperinas. To the left wheatfields stretched as
far as Taryn could see, the grain rustling, dipping, and
swaying at the whim of the wind that was still
blowing, although with its force abated somewhat by a
windbreak of sugar gums. On their right the land had
been significantly cleared also, but here stands of
shade-giving trees had been left to provide shelter for
the sheep that grazed the sown pastures.

Then, as they crested a slight rise a few minutes
later, Taryn found her gaze drawn to a tree-and-shrub
adorned area on the extending plain before them, the
various yards and outbuildings interspersed among
the greenery making it plain that they had finally
reached their destination.

The homestead itself wasn't visible until they had
passed a screening clump of trees, but once having
done so Taryn gave something of a gulp for its
generous size and stately proportions, and fell to
surveying it pensively. Built solidly from bluestone
with lighter contrasting quoins marking each corner

and window, it consisted of a central, two-storey block flanked on either side by large, matching, single storey wings, the whole encircled by a mosaic tiled verandah, complete with carefully arranged garden furniture and potted plants, that pleasingly linked all three sections. Immediately in front of the building a well-kept lawn was surrounded by a circular driveway, its edges bounded by obviously lovingly tended garden beds of brilliant annuals, while flowering shrubs of nearly every description ringed the verandah.

With a wry half smile, half grimace, Taryn guessed she should have expected Merringannee Bluff homestead to be something out of the ordinary, if only because of her brother's remarks about the family being members of the establishment squattocracy, but for some inexplicable reason it hadn't really featured much in her thoughts so that now, on recognising the undoubtedly dignified wealth it represented, she found herself speculating as to how on earth she was going to adapt to such a radical change in circumstances.

Why, a mere quarter of just one of those wings of the house could accommodate her parent's truck, caravan, ute, and trailer combined, and hardly know they were there! she mused drily, and not a little self-mockingly on alighting, once Slade had brought the station wagon to a halt beside the short flight of smoothly worn stone steps that led to the symmetrically carved front door with its attractively patterned lead-lighted side panels.

'I thought it may have been you when I heard the car so I came to bid you welcome,' an amiable, familiar voice suddenly declared and, turning, Taryn saw Jeff approaching along a path she presumed led to some of the outbuildings.

'Thank you,' she smiled at him gratefully. At the moment she felt decidedly in need of a friendly face.

'You could have knocked me over with a feather, though, when Slade told us that he'd hired you,' he continued in expressive accents. 'You never said anything to me about wanting to stay around here for a while . . . not even when we said goodbye.'

'No—well . . .' She shifted discomfitedly from one foot to the other as she tried to recall exactly what Slade had said he'd told his family. 'I—umm—it was really only something I had in the back of my mind until—until Slade mentioned there might be a vacancy here.'

'Oh?' His brows lifted and then lowered into a frown as he swung to look at his brother who was engaged in removing Taryn's case from the station wagon. 'But I thought you said Taryn approached *you* for work, not the other way round.'

Beside him, Taryn bit at her lip in dismay, her eyes wide and worried as they flew to Slade's tall form. Oh, Lord, she must have mixed their stories, after all!

For his part, Slade merely shrugged and asserted calmly, 'And so she did. Taryn was no doubt meaning that it still hadn't properly passed the idea stage until she knew for certain she was able to gain employment in the area.'

'Y-yes, that's quite right,' Taryn was swift to endorse, trying to ignore the distinctly less than favourable glance her new employer flashed graphically in her direction. 'Naturally, I couldn't make any firm decision until I could be sure there was work available.'

'I see,' nodded Jeff, accepting the explanation easily enough. 'Well, I for one, am very pleased with the way things have turned out, I can tell you,' with a smile.

'Good for you, old son!' put in Slade as he now joined them, his expression wryly mocking. 'However, I would just like to remind you that your girlfriend's here to work, not simply in order to keep you company. Get the message?'

If Jeff didn't, Taryn certainly did. In other words, he didn't intend for his brother to spend any more time with her than could possibly be prevented! Not that she considered herself the younger man's girlfriend, anyway! she added resentfully.

'Received and understood,' quipped Jeff good-naturedly, winking at Taryn. 'In the meantime, though . . .' It was he who began eyeing Slade tauntingly now. 'Mother's been anxiously awaiting your arrival in the sitting room . . . along with Ilona.'

'Ilona!' Slade stared at him askance. 'I thought you were going to drive her home on your way here last night.'

'So did I, but it appeared Mother had other ideas,' Jeff relayed with a broadening grin. 'She asked Ilona if she would care to stay the night here instead . . . and Ilona agreed, of course.'

'Of course!' Slade repeated, a corner of his shapely mouth slanting crookedly. 'When doesn't she fall in with whatever Mother suggests these days?' With Taryn's case in one hand, he motioned with the other for her to precede him towards the steps.

'Two females with byt a single aim,' Jeff laughed as he too began moving, but back along the path leading away from the homestead.

'Perhaps,' was all his brother was prepared to concede, but with such a subtle change in his demeanour that it immediately had Taryn studying him closely, if secretively.

Unless she was very much mistaken, that was

precisely the same indefinable look he'd had on his face the evening before when he'd finally agreed to employ her, and yet she still couldn't quite put her finger on just what the reason for it could be. Because now, more than ever, she was positive there was something he was keeping to himself—despite his words to the contrary made such a short while ago!

Nevertheless, as Slade opened the front door for her and Taryn moved into the spacious entrance hall beyond, she soon considered it judicious to leave that particular riddle for another time in order to concentrate all her attention on the meeting about to take place, She didn't wish to appear only partly interested on her very first day!

Depositing her case beside the first doorway on their left, Slade showed the way into the lofty sitting room and Taryn followed tensely. There was little opportunity for her to note much detail about the room except for the eye-catching white Italian marble mantelpiece topped by a eight-foot high burnished framed mirror that directly faced the doorway.

Of the remainder, she merely gained a brief impression of a highly polished escritoire and accompanying chair that rested alongside one of the three wide windows that illuminated the commodious room; an assortment of comfortably padded and proportioned armchairs; three large vase and lamp-bearing tables as well as a selection of individual side ones ... and a matching pair of leaf-green, velvet-covered sofas positioned on either side of the fireplace, upon one of which two women were seated.

The older of the two, Slade's mother obviously, was a slim, elegantly dressed woman in her late fifties with an imperious countenance, and an even more imperious manner of looking at you, Taryn discovered ruefully, for whereas her son's eyes were deep grey, hers were more of a piercing silver colour. The younger woman, who was certainly no less expensively attired, Taryn judged to be nearer to thirty than to twenty, her cleverly styled dark blonde hair contrasting attractively with a pair of dark brown eyes set in a finely featured face. Or should that be sharply featured? pondered Taryn on second thought, after having been the recipient of a narrow, unfriendly stare from the other girl.

'Darling! Surprise, surprise!' It was the younger woman who broke into bubbling—Taryn thought, affected—speech first as she swung a now somewhat coy glance in Slade's direction. 'You didn't expect to see me here today, did you?'

Slade inclined his head briefly. 'You're not wrong,' he conceded with a hint of wryness Taryn suspected the blonde missed completely, but which set her own lips twitching impulsively. Now she suspected she fully understood exactly what Jeff had meant by that last quip. It appeared the two seated women had marriage plans for her employer, but that, as yet—at least presumed so from what she'd seen and heard so far—he was proving reluctant in coming to the aid of the party. 'Since you are here, though,' he continued in a similar tone, 'it gives you the opportunity to meet my new offsider.' And drawing the girl beside him forward, 'Taryn, I'd like you to meet my mother, and a neighbour of ours, Ilona Welbourne. Taryn Rodgers,' he supplied in turn.

Murmuring a tentative, 'Mrs Douglas,' in response to the older woman's minimal nod of acknowledgment, Taryn wasn't allowed the time to do even that much with regard to Ilona, because that woman evidently had thoughts of her own she was more interested in voicing.

'*Your* offsider?' she burst out, her gaze anything but sweet now as it sought Slade's. 'I understood she was hired to help Bernadette with her committee work!'

Bernadette being Mrs Douglas, Taryn assumed. But in truth, she had been a little taken aback by his remark too. That wasn't what she believed her position was to be either!

And clearly, nor had it been his mother's if her chilly expression was any guide. 'As did I, Slade!' she now spoke up in a strongly accusing tone. 'In fact, I've already drawn up a considerable list of matters I thought . . .' she drew a plainly disapproving breath, 'Miss Rodgers could attend to this morning in order to save you the necessity of doing something similar yourself, and thereby permitting you to spend your time with Ilona instead.'

'For which thought I thank you,' Slade replied, drily smooth. 'However, I do think it would be a little more considerate if we gave Taryn the chance to at least unpack and have a look over the place before setting her to work, don't you?'

'Under the circumstances, I would have thought you'd already shown her sufficient consideration simply by employing her,' inserted Ilona in haughty accents. She uttered a brittle laugh. 'I mean, it's her brother who stole your money, so Bernadette tells me, and if one in the family is criminally inclined . . .' She left the sentence explicitly unfinished.

'Exactly!' Mrs Douglas had no compunction in stonily concurring. 'And what's more, I'm of the opinion that even if you did manage to get your money back, the matter should not have been allowed to stop there. You should have reported it to the police and had him charged with theft, anyway! These people apparently believe that because they're always on the move—just like a pack of vagrants,' with a depreciating shudder, 'they're not bound by the same laws that govern everyone else!'

Taryn's cheeks reddened at the deliberate disparagement, her hands clenching angrily at her sides. 'Itinerants maybe, Mrs Douglas, but definitely not vagrants!' she contradicted tightly. 'And although it may not provide such obvious rewards,' with a sardonic gaze taking in the well-endowed room about her, 'as some other occupations, it is still an honest living!'

'Yes, we can tell! Your brother's a good example!' smirked Ilona derisively.

'He's only one of many!' Taryn's defence came swiftly, hotly. Luke himself had made it impossible for her to justify his actions, but she wasn't about to weakly permit the rest of her family to be so accused, or the other honourable sideshow operators.

'One of many thieves?' The other girl's eyes widened mockingly.

'No! One of many who *do* have the decency and good amnners not to denigrate someone, and then merely because of association, the minute they set eyes on them! And that goes for you too!' Taryn rounded on Slade with equal vehemence as she spun on her heel and stormed from the room. To hell with all of them! There was no way she was going to work on this property!

'Well, really! I trust that's the last we'll see of her!' Mrs Douglas's censuring voice floated clearly into the entrance hall.

'I sincerely hope so!' followed Ilona's smug-sounding endorsement. 'It was quite obviously a mistake to have hired her at all!'

What Slade had to add to their comments Taryn couldn't distinguish, because by the time she heard him speak she had already heaved her suitcase into her hand and was three-quarters of the way to the front door. He was probably attempting to soothe their poor, tender feelings that she had so thoughtlessly ruffled, she grimaced bitterly as she flung open the door and hurried across the verandah.

'So where do you think you're headed?' She suddenly heard Slade enquire behind her, surprise that he wasn't still in the sitting room making her turn involuntarily to face him, despite being midway down the steps.

'Home!' she flared, just the thought of its uncomplicated serenity sufficient to have her eyes watering treacherously.

He raised an ironic brow. 'And the money you vowed to repay?'

She bit at her lip in despair, her slender shoulders sagging. Oh, God, how could she have forgotten, even temporarily in anger? Subconsciously, she must have been beginning to believe the story she had concocted for her parents. 'I—I'll send it to you in instalments as I—as I originally proposed,' she put forward dismally.

Slade gave a disallowing shake of his head. 'I told you before what I thought of that idea.'

Catching back a helpless sob, Taryn dropped her case on the verandah and sank down on the steps with her back to him, her fingers entwining agitatedly in her lap. 'Well, I'm not staying here to be humiliated by all and sundry at every turn!' she choked. 'It's not even as if I've done anything wrong!'

Looking at her fiery, downbent head, Slade rubbed a hand around the back of his neck and unexpectedly moved to sit beside her. 'I'm sorry,' he apologised on an oddly gruff note, surprising Taryn that he should have expressed any regrets at all. She had certainly never anticipated him doing anything of the kind where she was concerned. 'That wasn't the reception I either imagined or intended you to receive, but . . .' he lifted a hand in order to turn her disconsolate face towards him, 'I very much doubt there's any likelihood of something similar occurring again. I think that's the first time anyone's presumed to accuse my mother of lacking in manners and it came as something of a shock to her system, believe me!' His lips curved expressively.

'Well, she deserved it. They both did,' she maintained defensively, pulling away from his disturbing touch.

'As I also informed them.' He gave a short, ruefully accented laugh. 'Don't worry, I probably left them with even less doubts as to how I regarded their behaviour than you did.'

'You mean, you supported *me*?' Her long-lashed, violet eyes rounded in astonishment, and not a little pleasure.

'On this occasion I happened to consider you were right,' he smiled lazily.

Dismayed at the ungovernable manner in which her feelings had reacted merely because, for once, he hadn't found her at fault, Taryn now suppressed them determinedly. 'So who's to tell you the same when next *you* start making the same accusations?' she gibed.

'I was under the impression you were more than willing, and capable, in that area already,' he drawled.

'Except that you never believe a word I say in my defence,' with a moodily executed grimace.

'Nevertheless, I did still employ you.'

'According to you, only because that was the quickest, and most likely, method of having your money repaid! Not that you were all that keen on the idea, anyway, as I recall! That is, until—until . . .' She halted, the suspicion that he'd found it expedient for another reason also surfacing inexorably again. And as thought followed upon thought, 'I'd also like to know just why you introduced me as *your* offsider in there too!' Nodding sharply towards the house behind them. 'Because that was what started it all. Or was that the general idea? To do a little stirring?' A tinge of acid crept back into her voice.

Slade shrugged offhandedly. 'And why would I want to do that?'

'How should I know?' she countered, yet becoming more convinced by the minute that she was correct, his impassive-sounding enquiry notwithstanding, and in consequence she recklessly continued, 'Maybe because you haven't the courage to tell the pair of them you're not interested in their cosy little plans for your future, or perhaps you merely find it amusing to stir them a little before finally succumbing—just so you don't appear too easy to manipulate! But whatever the reason, you're not using me as the cat to put among the pigeons! Or in this instance should I say, the pigeon among the cats?' she quipped with smouldering sarcasm.

'Well, apart from the fact that my private life is absolutely no concern of yours, for your information, honey, I can assure you I don't allow myself to be manipulated into anything . . . by anyone!' he snapped right back. 'And nor do I require any supposedly unsuspecting pigeon to ensure I retain control of the situation! Not that the cats, as you put it, appeared to have escaped entirely unscathed from the encounter, anyway!'

Taryn hunched a slender shoulder diffidently, aware she was treading on thin ice. 'Then if that's the case, why *did* you introduce me as you did?' she still had to ask, but in a slightly more careful tone. 'You'd obviously told your mother differently, the same as you'd told me. So why the sudden change ... if it wasn't purely in order to provoke?'

'Try ... in order to protect!' he recommended in a caustic, rough-edged voice. 'Although I'm beginning to wonder if I should have bothered!'

'To protect ... whom?' Her expression turned to one of frowning bewilderment.

Slade released a long-suffering breath and shook his head exasperatedly. 'Oh, who do you think? You, of course!'

'M-me?' she stared at him even more confusedly. 'But why?'

'As I said, I'm beginning to wonder!'

'No, please!' She reached out a tentative hand to touch his arm. 'I don't understand any of this, and— and ...' She faltered to a stop, swallowing heavily, as he removed her hand from his sleeve but kept it clasped within his warm fingers as he appeared to study it contemplatively.

'You do hard work with your hands,' he mused, running a finger over her upturned palm.

Taryn nodded weakly, unable to speak because of the lump that seemed to have become lodged in her throat. His hands were strong but gentle, his touch disconcerting and yet somehow comforting too, and if she was honest with herself she knew she'd admit that she really didn't want to speak in case it shattered the mood that suddenly seemed to bind them.

'Mother wouldn't approve of that either,' he continued drily. 'And unfortunately, my mother can be one formidable lady if she happens to take against someone.' Taryn was inclined to think she would be that at any time, but remained silent. 'So having a suspicion that's exactly what she had done where you're concerned even before meeting you, and guessing the manner in which she was likely to vent her antipathy—as you heard, she'd think nothing of loading you with so much work that you wouldn't see the outside of the homestead from one month to the next—I figured the best way to ensure she couldn't attempt to commandeer all your time was to inform her right at the start that as far as I was concerned you were here to help me, and therefore you would only be working for her when I didn't require you.' He turned to eye her wryly. 'Now do you understand?'

She nodded again, self-consciously, still all-too aware he hadn't yet released her hand.

'Only you're not sure which one of us is the lesser evil, hmm?' Slade suddenly drawled tauntingly.

'Oh, no, I'd much rather work for you,' she blurted spontaneously, unthinkingly. Then, blushing hotly, and not wanting him to think it was for any personal reason, tried to cover herself. 'I—I mean, I've always worked outside, and—and naturally I'd prefer to continue doing so if at all possible.'

'Naturally,' he concurred, but on such a mocking note that her face immediately flamed anew. At last setting her hand free, he rose to his feet in a smooth, fluid action while Taryn thrust both her hands into the pockets of her parka as if to prevent any possible recapture of either of them. 'So would you like to see your new charges?' He glanced down at her questioningly.

'Yes, very much,' she assented, rising upright too, and striving to appear as unaffected by that strange interlude as he evidently had been. And as she kept pace with him along the path that led to the rear of the homestead, 'And—and thank you for trying to stop—to stop . . .' She paused, at something of a loss as to just how to express her feelings in the right terms.

'To stop my mother from making your life a misery?' Slade apparently had no such reservations.

'I—I guess so,' she owned awkwardly, and changed the subject swiftly. 'How many dogs do you have at the moment, then?'

'About thirty-odd,' he advised with a shrug. 'Although ten of those are pups from two recent litters. Those being the ones you'll be looking after.'

Taryn thought she liked the sound of that, and on reaching the compound where the dogs were kept behind the gardens at the back of the house, smiled to hear the vociferous welcome they were accorded from all the animals kennelled there. Some were obviously fully grown working dogs, others still maturing, but it was the scampering, bounding, leap-frogging pups that caught and held her interest, as well as made her laugh when Slade opened the door to their exercise yard and they came flying towards them, all knobbly legs, floppy ears, and wet tongues.

'Oh, aren't they gorgeous,' she smiled as she impulsively sat down on the grass beside them and was promptly attacked by a mass of excited, squirming, furry little bodies, every one doing its best to clamber higher and higher upon her. Picking up one particularly persistent one, she buried her face in its soft coat playfully, and was rewarded with a series of wet licks to her ear. 'Well, at least it's nice to know that someone round here doesn't seem to find me all that terrible,' she quipped, albeit a trifle wistfully.

'Mmm, but then dogs don't know anything about money, and what some people are willing to do for it, do they?' Slade retorted above her.

Taryn kept her head bowed, her eyes misting uncontrollably. So much for thinking, hoping, that his support of her against his mother and girlfriend may have indicated he was revising his opinion of her. It appeared it hadn't altered one iota, after all.

CHAPTER FOUR

By the end of her first fortnight on Merringannee, Taryn was starting to become a little more accustomed to being employed by someone other than her father, and even to enjoy some aspects of her new employment. To have a room all to herself, and especially one of the generous size the Douglas homestead only appeared to consist of, she found a real luxury after always having shared a rather cramped caravan with her family previously. Also, she derived a great deal of pleasure from her work with the dogs, although the same unfortunately couldn't be said about the time, small though it was in comparison, that she spent indoors at the beck and call of Mrs Douglas.

In that regard, her work mostly revolved around typing the older woman's notes, for her various meetings, as well as making numerous phone calls to arrange such functions since Bernadette Douglas seemed to be either the secretary or the president of so many of the district's organisations, but as Taryn was neither a trained typist nor familiar with the various members and their associated roles, it more often than not took her some considerable time to complete all the work given her—much to Mrs Douglas's unconcealed and intolerant displeasure.

A circumstance that still wouldn't have worried Taryn to a great extent, surmising that she could hopefully only improve with practise, if it hadn't been for the constant complaints concerning her ability, or inadequacy thereof, that Slade was almost triumphantly regaled with by his mother on each such occasion.

It made it all too painfully apparent, to Taryn at least, that the older woman was no more resigned to her presence on the property than she had been initially and, in consequence, it didn't really come as all that much of a surprise to her when, shortly into her third week, she was summoned, all unsuspecting at the time, before Mrs Douglas and Slade in the library one evening.

'I'd like to know if you were in my mother's bedroom today.' It was Slade who began in a curt voice as soon as she was seated.

'Well—yes, I was actually, I'm sorry,' Taryn confirmed, albeit discomfitedly, knowing the room to be out of bounds of her, and with an apologetic look in his mother's direction. 'Not because I . . .'

'There! You see, I wasn't mistaken! I told you I'd seen her sneaking out of my room when she thought no one was looking!' Bernadette Douglas interjected on a distinctly jubilant note. 'Although I must say I didn't expect her to have the effrontery to admit it quite so brazenly!' She took a deep breath, eyeing her son peremptorily. 'I warned you what would happen if you were foolish enough to insist on hiring someone of her kind! Now perhaps you'll concede that I was correct and report the matter to the authorities accordingly!'

Report her to the authorities! For having entered a room without permission? Taryn could only stare from one to the other of them, perplexed. It sounded improbable in the extreme, and yet knowing just how much Mrs Douglas would dearly love to see her dismissed, it made her decidedly apprehensive all the same.

Slade, meanwhile, gave a short shake of his head. 'A rather pointless exercise without more definite proof,' he counselled.

'Well, you will at least fire her immediately, I hope!'

When he didn't reply straight away, Taryn, who had already edged forward anxiously on her seat, her nerves tensing unbelievably as a result of his previous remark, took the opportunity to demand the clarification, 'Proof of what?'

'Oh, don't think you can squirm out of it by feigning innocence now!' his mother broke in once more to deride. 'It's a little late for that in view of your already having confessed to creeping in to the room—where you had no reason to be, isn't it?'

'Except that I didn't creep in there! I walked in quite openly,' Taryn retorted defensively. 'And you still haven't explained . . . proof of what?' She fixed her gaze squarely, defiantly almost, on Slade.

'My mother's missing a pair of diamond earrings . . .'

'An extremely valuable pair of diamond earrings . . . as if you didn't know!' inserted Mrs Douglas sharply.

'That apparently disappeared from a jewel case in her room some time between shortly after breakfast and lunch today,' he concluded grimly.

'And you think I took them?' Taryn gasped incredulously, and not a little indignantly.

'*Stole* them!' amended Mrs Douglas with pungent emphasis.

'But—but I was only in there for a few seconds, and I certainly didn't go anywhere near the jewel case!'

'Then why were you in there?' Slade challenged coldly, his narrowed glance unswerving.

'Be-because your mother sent me upstairs to her study next door in order to fetch a particular list of names she required, only the door was locked, so rather than waste time by going all the way downstairs again to ask for the key I thought it would be all right if, just that once, I slipped through her bedroom to the study instead,' Taryn relayed earnestly.

Mrs Douglas gave vent to a scornful half laugh. 'The study door locked! Can't you think of something more plausible than that? No doors in this house are ever locked—they've never had to be. Our staff have always been totally trustworthy . . . until now!'

Doing her best to disregard that last denigrating comment, Taryn kept her eyes pinned on the man facing her. He was the only one she could appeal to, in spite of his sentiments concerning herself seemingly coinciding with his parent's so often, and for some strange reason it was important to her that he, more than anyone, believed her innocent.

'But it was locked!' she insisted. 'And besides, they're not the sort of thing I'd be likely to wear, anyway! Nor would it be much use in my taking them with the thought of selling them later when expensive jewellery,' particularly the kind that Mrs Douglas wore, 'is so easy to identify . . . and trace!'

Slade flexed a muscular shoulder. 'So maybe you've some debts you'd like to clear in a hurry, and were therefore willing to take that gamble,' he put forward meaningfully.

Taryn continued to hold his gaze for a moment, then dropped her lavender eyes desolately, blinking rapidly to clear the mist that had abruptly veiled them. It seemed she was to be convicted on her brother's record once again. 'And perhaps they haven't been stolen at all, but Mrs Douglas has simply mislaid them somewhere,' she suggested in a low voice.

'Mislaid them!' the older woman promptly expostul-

ated, her expression one of mocking contempt.
'Jewellery doesn't become *mislaid* in a jewel case, Miss
Rodgers, and that is precisely where I saw them last at
nine-thirty this morning! No, to disappear as they did,
someone has to have taken them, and as soon as I saw
you leaving my room in such a guilty fashion I knew
without a doubt that you had been up to no good!'

'Then if that was the case, why didn't you say
something to me about it at the time?' Taryn
countered, curiosity uppermost, notwithstanding that
vexing exaggeration of her having a supposedly guilty
appearance. Something didn't make sense here. Since
she had gone to fetch the list Mrs Douglas had
wanted, there had been no reason for the other woman
to be upstairs at that particular time, anyway. 'Surely,
if you had, that would have enabled you to catch me
red-handed . . . *if* I'd had anything of yours on me.
Why wait until so late in the day before even
mentioning the matter?'

Bernadette Douglas's silvery eyes flashed brightly.
'Because I wished to advise my son of the appalling
incident first, of course! Not that I realised you had
actually dared to deal something, despite your furtive
manner, until some time this afternoon, as it so
happens! However, I'll have you know that I'm not
here to answer any of your evidently, hopefully
diverting questions, my girl, but that you're here
solely to answer ours!' She paused, her mouth taking
on a scornful curve. 'And to date you haven't been at
all convincing, I can assure you!'

Neither had she concerning the *loss* of her earrings,
thought Taryn abruptly. In fact, not once so far had
the other woman shown any particular wish to recover
her missing jewellery at all! Her whole desire seeming
to be centred on obtaining the termination of Taryn's

employment. And that being so, it promptly gave rise
to the suspicion that perhaps her earrings hadn't
disappeared after all. She merely found it expedient to
make such a claim purely as a means to have Taryn
dismissed.

'Then why not search my room if you're so positive
I have them?' she consequently challenged impulsively,
then immediately drew in a strangled breath of
consternation. If Mrs Douglas was prepared to go to
such lengths to have her fired, it was also more than
probable that she would have planted her jewellery in
Taryn's room as proof of her allegation.

'Oh, what would be the use?' Bernadette Douglas
unexpectedly waved aside the idea disdainfully. 'You
could have hidden them anywhere by now—outside
the house even—and not finding them wouldn't prove
anything.'

'Except maybe my innocence!' Taryn shot back in
sardonic overtones, sure now that her suspicion had
been correct. Mrs Douglas could afford not to display
any worry regarding her supposed loss. She had never
intended to allow her earrings to leave her possession
in the first place! 'And without any proof that I have
them, I hardly see you've any grounds for having me
sacked!'

'A pertinent point, Mother, you must admit,'
conceded Slade expressionlessly, and much to Taryn's
surprise. Since he really hadn't had much to say on the
matter—and what he had said hadn't particularly filled
her with confidence—she had assumed he was
wholeheartedly in accord with his parent's aims.

Clearly his mother must have believed so too,
because she now looked somewhat taken aback,
though only momentarily, and then she pressed her
lips together vexedly. 'I admit no such thing!' she

napped. 'The only pertinent point as I see it, is that he should be dismissed instantly! What more proof of er guilt do you need than that I *saw* her leaving my oom?'

'And I've already explained why I was there!' 'aryn's reminder was urgently voiced.

'Yes, we know! Some inconceivable story about the tudy supposedly being locked!'

'Well, maybe the door was just stuck, then!' An ntreating amethyst gaze was sent in Slade's direction. All I know is, I couldn't open it!'

His return glance was inscrutable. 'No one's ever ad any trouble with it before,' he shrugged.

'Precisely!' endorsed his mother, while Taryn's opes slumped again. 'So now I trust we can bring his whole extremely unpleasant and disturbing pisode to its appropriate conclusion, and thereby ermit us to enjoy again the agreeable and trusting tmosphere that existed here before Miss Rodgers' sly ttempts to ingratiate herself with both you and efferson in an obvious effort to attract the interest of t least one, if not both of you, brought such disruptive ension and distress into the household!'

'That's not true!' refuted Taryn swiftly, thankful to know that Slade at least was all too aware of the true eason for her presence there. But it did explain xactly why Mrs Douglas was so anxious to see her ismissed. Unaccountably, she appeared to think 'aryn presented some threat to her plans for Slade nd Ilona, and if her apprehension hadn't expressed tself in such a dire form, the younger girl would have ound her anxieties amusing. After all, Slade's opinion of her was only a little less condemning than his nother's, and as for Jeff . . . well, they merely found each other's company pleasant, nothing more.

In the meantime, Mrs Douglas simply responded to the denial with a sound of scoffing disbelief and eyed her son expectantly.

With one ankle raised and supported across his opposite knee, his elbows resting on the arms of his chair, Slade rested his chin on his upraised and clasped hands and exhaled heavily. 'I'm sorry, but no I'm not going to fire her,' he finally gave his decision on an unequivocal note. 'In my opinion, there isn't sufficient proof to warrant such action, and therefore I believe Taryn's entitled to the benefit of the doubt.'

For a moment silence reigned supreme, and it would have been difficult to say who was the most astonished at the outcome, Taryn or Mrs Douglas, but while Taryn gave a heartfelt sigh of relief, the older woman's sharp inhalation was more like a gasp of incredulity.

'You mean, you're taking *her* word against mine? Your own mother!' she protested censoriously. 'But then, right from her first day here she's had you turning against your family and friends, hasn't she?'

'No, of course not,' Slade disclaimed in mild exasperation. 'In any event, that was something else entirely.'

'Was it?' came the stinging dispute. 'And what about her insolence and insubordination when you're not here to see it, then? Are you expecting me to put up with a continuation of that also?'

His brows drew together sharply in a frown. 'You've never mentioned anything about this before.'

'Because there's not a word of truth in it, that's why! inserted Taryn fierily. God, what wasn't the woman prepared to invent in order to get her own way? 'Not once have I ever ...'

'Leave it, Taryn!' Slade suddenly ordered peremptorily, cutting her off.

'No!' she defied indignantly. 'I'm not going to . . .'

'You'll do as you're damn well told, and I said . . . *leave it!*' There was a decided grate to his voice this time that had her prudently, but huffily, doing as instructed.

'You see, that's exactly what I've had to contend with as well!' Mrs Douglas pounced on the opportunity to confirm her previous claim with patent satisfaction. 'But even if it wasn't, I could never trust her working in the house again. I would only worry myself sick every time she was out of sight, wondering what was going to disappear next.'

'Hmm . . .' Slade mused meditatively, even as Taryn fumed over this last aspersion. 'Then I guess there's only one way to solve both problems, isn't there?'

'And that is?' questioned his mother, not bothering to disguise her eagerness as she obviously anticipated having her wishes complied with at last.

Taryn simply swallowed, hard, dismayed to think her own impetuous outburst may have finally been the turning point in the older woman's favour.

'I'll just have to ensure Taryn is with me all the time so I can keep an eye on her,' Slade proposed on a decisive note, and once again managing to amaze both his listeners.

'I see,' his mother acknowledged icily and rose to her feet. 'As I said, you're obviously allowing her to influence you against your own family, and I can only be thankful your father isn't alive to witness such reprehensible behaviour. It's the type of action I may have expected from your brother, Slade, but I certainly never anticipated you taking such a stand. Nevertheless, I still have hopes of you regaining your senses before too long—I've no doubt Miss Rodgers

will be unable to avoid revealing her true colours,
even to you—and then perhaps you'll be willing to
admit that I was right all along and that there's no
place for her here!' And with one last, infinitely
disapproving glare at Taryn she swept regally from
the room.

'I'm sorry,' murmured Taryn on a diffident note as
soon as the door was closed again.

'For what? Making a difficult task even harder by
refusing to keep quiet?' Slade mocked sarcastically as
he too swung out of his chair and moved to stand
beside the fireplace, one arm resting on the mantel as
he looked back at her.

'Oh!' Her violet-blue eyes smouldered with resentment. 'Well, what was I supposed to do? Meekly
accept everything that was said about me when it just
wasn't true?'

'That could have been preferable than your efforts
to presumably give them substance!'

'So how was I to know if you'd believe them or not
if I didn't defend myself?'

'Since you're always claiming I never believe what
you have to say, anyway, I'm surprised you bothered!
And if you recall, I told you to leave it,' he reminded
abrasively.

'Oh, great! He told me to leave it,' she mimicked in
caustic accents. 'For all I knew that could have
meant—leave it, because I don't believe a word you
say—or even, leave it, because I want to hear all my
mother's accusations first!' Pausing, she pressed her
lips together fractiously. 'And what's more, I don't
think you're being fair in taking it out on me just
because your mother isn't very happy with *you* at the
moment!'

Unexpectedly, that brought forth a warm and totally

free laugh from his bronzed throat. 'She's even unhappier with you,' he drawled, wryly.

Taryn caught at her lower lip with shining white teeth. 'I know,' she nodded miserably, and cast him an anxious glance. 'But I didn't take her earrings! I swear I didn't!'

Slade dragged a hand through his dark hair, giving it an attractively tousled look. 'No, I know you didn't,' he owned on a deep, half-sighed half-rasped note.

Never having anticipated him believing her, Taryn could only stare at him in stunned surprise for a few seconds. 'You mean, you knew right from the beginning?' she hazarded at length.

'No, not then.' He gave a brief shake of his head. But with his shapely mouth starting to quirk, 'When you challenged us to search your room, and then promptly looked horrified at having suggested anything of the sort.'

She hadn't realised he'd noticed her rapid change of demeanour. 'Initially, I thought it was the only hope I had of proving my innocence, but once I'd said it I immediately thought that if—if someone,' she was reluctant to actually point the finger at his mother, 'wanted it to appear as if—as if I was guilty, then they could easily have—have . . .' She faltered to an uncomfortable stop, even more unwilling to voice the underhanded tactics she believed his mother had attempted to utilise.

'Hidden the earrings in your room without you being aware of it?' Slade concluded for her bluntly. And without waiting for, or apparently requiring her verification, went on, 'Exactly as I interpreted your action to mean.'

'You did?' she quizzed wonderingly, her surprise at his perspicacity plain to see. 'But how?'

He shrugged indolently. 'It wasn't particularly difficult. I simply figured you would hardly suggest we search your room if you did have something hidden there, while at the same time, if you had them somewhere else then there was certainly no reason for that dismayed look that came over your face immediately afterwards. So, putting two and two together, I merely deduced that the only circumstance that could have generated both such reactions was if you had absolutely no idea at all where the earrings were.'

'I suppose your mother must have mislaid them, after all,' she put forward hesitantly. Maybe it was a possibility.

'Mmm, mislaid them somewhere known only to herself, no doubt!' His voice hardened roughly. 'And for God's sake, spare me the pretence of you supposedly thinking otherwise! Do you think I'm that simple I couldn't tell what she was up to?'

'No, I don't think you're simple!' Anything but, in fact! 'But I still wasn't to know just how aware you were, was I?' Taryn flared, springing upright herself now. 'So there's no call for you to start venting your annoyance on me again just because I was trying to make certain I hadn't jumped to the wrong conclusion! You could do worse than try it yourself sometime instead of always thinking the worst of people!'

'People . . . or you?'

Flustered by his directness, as well as a particular nuance she thought she detected in his tone, she lowered her gaze protectively. 'I—well—you could be a little less suspicious of everything I say and do, couldn't you?'

'I was under the impression I already had been by

not believing either allegation Mother made about you tonight,' drily.

'Then for that I—I thank you,' she stammered self-consciously, knowing her timing had been unfortunate for making such a complaint. 'And I'm sorry to have been the cause of trouble between you and your mother. It never occurred to me my working here would create such friction.'

A wry slant tilted his lips crookedly. 'I thought it more than probable.'

'Because of my connection with—with Luke?'

He shrugged. 'Originally, maybe, but I'd say not especially since she met you.'

'Due to my outspokenness the day I arrived, I suppose,' she sighed.

'Oh, for crying out loud!' he suddenly startled her by exclaiming harshly, and before she knew it had caught hold of her by the nape of the neck and propelled her towards the mirror above the mantel-piece. 'No! Due to *that*, of course!'

Taryn stared back at her reflection mechanically. She may not have been vain about her looks, but it had never been possible for her to be unaware of them either, and recalling her own observations from only a short time before regarding Mrs Douglas's unfounded reasons for wanting her dismissed, she pulled a grimacing expression and heaved glumly, 'My face.'

Watching her, Slade smiled lazily. 'Your very beautiful face,' he qualified in ironic tones.

That he should find her so had Taryn's senses leaping ungovernably, but only for a second before she subdued them again determinedly. Turning away from the mirror, she forced herself to face him as dispassionately as she could. 'Well, perhaps if you explained to her . . .'

'What?' he interposed, his brows sweeping upwards to a sardonic peak. 'That she has nothing to fear because I'm immune to such stunning features?'

'Well, since you undoubtedly are . . .'

'Am I?' His slate grey eyes took in a darkening hue as his head inclined disturbingly closer.

Taryn licked at her lips agitatedly, only just realising that their nearness was a result of the hand that still rested at her nape, and tried, unsuccessfully, to take a few composing steps backwards. 'W-well, naturally,' she half laughed unsteadily, breathlessly, and suddenly feeling warmer than the size of the fire in the grate beside her justified.

'Then maybe you can explain why I've felt like doing this for some time now,' he drawled, lightly mocking, and pulling her firmly against his rugged frame his descending mouth took possession of hers with a speed and mastery that left her gasping.

Lord, but the man could kiss! was her first compulsive, totally disconcerting thought as she felt herself beginning to respond helplessly to the persuasive demand of his sensuous lips. Instead of making an effort to evade the burning contact, she found herself unconsciously wanting to prolong it, her slender form already moulding itself pliantly to the virile masculinity of his, her hands first clutching and then pressing at his sides as if uncertain whether to urge him still nearer or push him away. Then, all of a sudden, reason, awareness, discernment, returned in a rush of self-consciousness—didn't she have enough problems already without foolishly inviting more in this perturbing fashion?—and catching him offguard, she wrested herself free in something of a flurry.

'I—I think you're confusing me with—with Ilona,' she charged shakily, just the mention of the other girl's name thankfully enabling her to regain some of her lost composure. 'Moreover, all things considered, I also think it would be better if everything was kept on a—a purely business footing during my time here.'

Dipping his head slightly, wryly, Slade slanted her a chafing, sidelong glance that had her eyeing him warily. 'Provided it's possible, of course.'

'I see no reason why it shouldn't be,' Taryn asserted, if rather stiltedly, as she desperately tried to discount her too-recent traitorous lapse in control as well as those other occasions when he had somehow managed to have such an inexplicable effect on her emotions. 'And particularly since your mother would definitely prefer you to reserve any such—such attentions for someone else entirely.'

'No doubt.' Strong, white teeth sparkled behind an indolent grin. 'Except that no one, least of all my mother, makes those decisions for me!' He took a quick step forward, one hand snaking out to span her chin and tip her face up to his disquietingly. 'And just to keep the record straight, no man in his right mind could ever confuse you with Ilona, honey. You're in a class of your own.'

As was he! The unbidden thought promptly followed to Taryn's dismay, and irritation, in view of her having only just attempted to rid herself of any such discomposing observations. To overcome it, she forced a facetious smile on to her lips. 'Mmm, I know—the socially unacceptable, not to be trusted, working class!' she quipped.

'That isn't what I meant, and you know it,' he denied, contemplating her with lazy speculation. 'And nor have I ever said—or implied—that you were socially unacceptable either.'

'Just not to be trusted, huh?'

With his hand still capturing her chin, Slade simply tilted her head a little further backwards and claimed her lips once more for a brief, but undeniably thorough moment. 'Perhaps not ... when your lips immediately renounce any such statements are a purely business relationship the minute you're kissed,' he drawled expressively in finally releasing her.

Taryn spun away from him, embarrassed, her cheeks aflame with colour, her senses in disarray, knowing she couldn't possibly gainsay his claim because she was only too aware that her mouth had indeed waywardly responded to the intoxication of his once again. In lieu, she lifted her head to a higher elevation and parried, 'It's been a rather distracting evening, and—and I'm probably not reacting to things in the way I normally would as yet.'

'If that's the result, I think I'd prefer it if you never did,' he bantered with a smile twitching at the corner of his mouth.

He was laughing at her because he knew damned well it was nothing of the sort! Taryn despaired, and doubled her efforts to make it appear otherwise. 'More than likely,' she rejoined crisply. 'None the less, I suggest you content yourself with Ilona all the same, because I can assure you I've no intention of conveniently making myself available on those occasions when she happens to be elsewhere!'

'How inconsiderate of you!' His own voice firmed now, but with a sarcastic inflection. 'Particularly when I don't even remember asking you to.'

'I—umm—I simply didn't want you perhaps labouring under a misapprehension, that's all,' she excused, flushing, but refusing to drop her gaze.

In turn, his smoky grey and alert eyes held hers mockingly. 'I wasn't aware that I was.'

Taryn gulped. 'You're talking in circles,' she scoffed, suspecting he spoke no more than the truth, but still trying desperately not to let it show.

'While you're running scared!'

'Oh, that's r-ridiculous!' she retorted, seeking protection in anger now, albeit a mite shakily. 'What have I to be scared about?'

'As to that, I guess only time will tell, won't it?'

And time, spent in *his* company, was what she was about to have even more of than she had previously, she abruptly recollected. 'Mmm, I suppose it will,' she just managed to push out with a creditable display of indifference, and made for the door smartly before he could add anything else.

That was, anything else besides his amused-sounding taunt, 'Starting from the usual time at the kennels tomorrow, hmm?'

Not trusting herself to speak, mainly because she was too nervous of extending their increasingly perturbing conversation if she did so, Taryn merely nodded and hastily took her leave.

He had charged her with being scared, she mused with a sinking feeling as she made her way up the stairs to her room—and he was right. Oh, God, was she scared! Scared, because she couldn't fathom just why he should have adopted such a changed attitude towards her, and scared, perhaps most alarmingly of all, because if he did take it into his head to kiss her again, she was all too aware there was a distinct possibility she might not find the willpower, or the desire, to break free at all next time!

CHAPTER FIVE

THE following morning after breakfast—an early meal Taryn always shared with Slade and Jeff in the homestead's large kitchen rather than with Mrs Douglas who usually preferred to have hers at a slightly later hour in the dining room—Taryn was still in something of a nervous state as she accompanied Slade down to the kennels.

It wasn't that he had made any reference to the events of the previous evening, or even voiced any mocking insinuations concerning them, if it came to that—as she had been half expecting him to do—but the knowledge of those last perturbing, for her at least, moments was clearly there between them all the same, she realised, and although he seemed able to accept the situation with an indolent equanimity, she found her own feelings nowhere near as composed, despite her valiant efforts to make them appear so.

Consequently, as soon as they left the homestead behind, she attempted to keep up a hopefully disguising, as well as diverting, conversation regarding the particular dogs they would be working with that morning, but as her helplessly stiff words only succeeded in eliciting some very askance glances along with his responses—humorously askance, at that, she suspected in dismayed mortification—she eventually decided it would be better if she settled for a merely inwardly discomfited silence after all.

Not so Slade, evidently, for as they reached the youngest pups' yard he promptly quizzed on a wryly explicit note, 'Do you always react in such an edgy fashion just because you've been kissed? Or is it simply the thought of what might happen should something similar occur again that worries you so much?'

'No!' she lied with a heavy swallow. He was too close to the truth for her peace of mind, and especially when her whole intent had originally been to convince him that her agitation of the night before was now a thing of the past. 'As it so happens, that doesn't afford me any worries at all.' Then, realising just how that could be construed by the goading, brow-raised look she received as a result, stammered defensively, 'Because nothing similar *will* be occurring, of course!' Her lavender eyes lifted to his bravely in a last desperate show of denial. 'Nor do I feel in the least edgy, as you put it, either!'

His ensuing, openly disbelieving laugh had Taryn's honey skinned cheeks colouring with a humiliated warmth. 'You could have fooled me!' he mocked.

'And apparently did, obviously!' she just managed to force herself into quipping, bittersweetly. No matter how embarrassed or disconcerted she felt, she still had to protect herself somehow.

Once again, Slade's brows flicked eloquently high. 'You reckon?' came the immediate, drily voiced retaliation.

'I've just said so, haven't I?' she countered with a grimace of pseudo-exasperation, as if unable to understand his continuing allegations to the contrary. Succeeded by a hasty, and optimistically distracting, 'But now, if you've quite finished with all your rather amusingly distorted delusions, I might suggest we begin paying some attention to these little fellows before they do actually manage to pull this wire to pieces in their efforts to reach us.' And she sank down on to her haunches to start patting the pups in the yard beside them, who until then, had indeed been doing their utmost to destroy the barrier that was keeping them penned.

'I know who's deluding their self, honey,' Slade drawled lazily as he opened the door to the yard. 'But if that's the way you're determined to have it, it's okay by me.' A pause. 'For the moment, anyhow.'

Uncertain as to just what he was implying, and even less sure she really wanted to know, Taryn chose to concentrate her attention on the half-dozen pups that were now leaping about them excitedly, and so avoid answering at all. She figured it was probably the most prudent course for her to take.

Meanwhile, the pups—a couple red, a couple black, the other two a combination of both colours—continued to dance about their legs until they each picked up three, whereupon there were then subjected to enthusiastic licks as they carried the ten-week old bundles down to the small yard where three or four quiet, old ewes had been mustered the night before. Today was the first time they would be actually let loose with any sheep and Taryn was extremely interested to see their reaction.

During the past couple of weeks she had watched on many occasions when Slade had been training some of the older ones, teaching them the commands they would immediately obey throughout their working lives whether the signals were made by voice, hand, or in the form of a whistle, but because she had more or less had sole charge over them since arriving on the property she somehow felt closer to, and more involved with, the pups who were starting out today.

The sheep were clustered together at one end of the yard when they entered and seeing Slade put his charges to the ground, Taryn did the same. It wasn't the first occasion the pups had been close to sheep, of course. For the last week Taryn had been bringing them down to the race one at a time to accustom them to at first just sitting on the sheep's backs in order to build their confidence as a forerunner to the time when they would be required to run across the animals with uncanny balance and no hesitation whatever should it become necessary for them to clear a jam in the race, or simply to keep them moving in equally confined areas, as well as allowing each dog to sniff and, naturally lick, at the larger animals in their normal way of becoming acquainted with new objects.

Once on the ground, though, it was possible to see their inherited instincts coming to the fore almost immediately, because they promptly pranced off towards the sheep while Slade and Taryn followed behind. The first to reach them was Red, one of the males in the litter, who on seeing the sheep nervously turn to face him, immediately dropped to a half crouch and, even at that tender age, succeeded in keeping the animals exactly where they were by the use of his eyes only. 'Eye,' as it was called, was an almost mesmerising glare kelpies used to convince sheep it was in their best interests to remain exactly where they were, and one of the fundamental characteristics that made the breed so invaluable, as Taryn had discovered, but to see a pup so young utilising it instinctively still came as something of a surprise to her and she turned impulsively with a smile to the man beside her.

'That looks promising, doesn't it?' she said.

'Mmm,' agreed Slade slowly, without taking his

eyes from the dog. 'Provided he doesn't think that's all he needs to do.'

As if on cue the pup now began to move around the back of the sheep, his action giving the man observing him cause to nod with satisfaction. '*Now* he looks promising,' he endorsed.

'Why, in particular, because he moved behind them?' Taryn asked interestedly.

'Because that's the way they keep a mob of sheep on the move—by continually masking half-circling movements behind them,' he explained. 'It's good that he can stop them breaking away by using his eyes, but his main task is to keep those animals moving steadily in the direction you want them to go, and he won't be able to do that just by staring at them.'

'I see.' She nodded her understanding and returned her attention to the pups.

The rest of them had reached the sheep as well now, and it was incredible to see how they appeared to know automatically what they were supposed to do, for now the sheep did start breaking away, but each time they did one or other of the pups would immediately set off after them and herd them all together again.

As Taryn and Slade moved closer, however, not surprisingly in view of their age, the dogs started to lose some of their interest in the sheep and, running back towards the two of them, began dancing about their legs again as they followed them round the yard. Soon, they seemed to be trailing Taryn almost exclusively and she started to smile.

'Why me?' she enquired of Slade humorously.

His answering grin had her breath catching in her throat as she tried to subdue her treacherously responding emotions. 'Since you feed them, I suspect you represent dinner,' he advised drily.

'Oh! I see,' she laughed, if a little unsteadily, and bent to pick up one of the pups. 'So your affections can be bought that easily, hmm?' With a mock reproving smile for the ecstatic form in her arms.

'Only at this age, though,' qualified Slade indolently. 'Once they're working and have confidence in their owner, you couldn't ask for higher fidelity from an animal. They become real one-man dogs.'

Taryn digested the information thoughtfully. 'Doesn't that make it difficult, then, when you sell them?'

'Not really.' He shook his head in a lightly negating gesture. 'Apart from the fact that most of them are still quite young when they're sold—trained, but without having started work in earnest—it is true what they say about the breed that they'd rather work than eat, so whoever puts them to work has their allegiance.' He paused. 'And since a large percentage of our orders these days are repeats, I guess you could say it was a fair indication their predecessors have been found to be most satisfactory.'

A more than fair recommendation, she conceded. 'They don't only work sheep, though, do they?' she queried next. She had often seen them on cattle properties along the road as they passed.

'Uh-uh!' His confirmation was laconically decisive. 'They're capable of herding just about any animal there is—as their export record shows. In Hawaii they're used with pigs, in the U.S. and Canada with sheep and cattle, in Kuwait with goats, and in Lapland with reindeer—just to name a few.'

'Lapland!' she exclaimed in surprise. 'You mean, they've even heard of them that far away?'

Slade's lips twitched wryly. 'You'd probably be surprised at just how many, and how diverse, are the countries that have come to recognise the kelpie's worth.'

'For example?'

'Kenya, Holland, Mexico, Scotland, Israel,' he supplied casually. 'Plus, there's over a couple of hundred of them in Sweden alone now.'

Taryn moved her head incredulously. 'Heavens! I knew there was hardly a grazier in Australia who didn't have at least one of them, but I certainly never imagined so many others knew of them too.' Her eyes rose to his enquiringly. 'Are they expensive to buy?' Abruptly remembering it was the proceeds of some such sales that her brother had relieved him of at the show.

'Not especially,' he shrugged. 'And definitely not when you take into consideration that when mustering and yarding sheep one dog is capable of doing the work of six men ... whose wages would equal the price of a fully trained, mature dog within a couple of months, whereas aside from the cost of his feed, you'll get ten or twelve years work out of the dog for that single, original outlay.'

'I'm beginning to understand now why there's only you, Jeff, and Burt Albright,' the property's sole stockman, whose wife acted as housekeeper, 'running Merringannee Bluff,' she half smiled ruefully. And looking down at the pup she still held, and which had hardly stopped bathing her neck and cheek with a wet, pink tongue since she picked it up, 'So how much would Penny here cost?'

'As she is now—around four hundred or so.'

'And Ace?' she quizzed slyly, naming the fully grown dog that was his most appreciated and respected specimen. A more perfect example of the breed she knew it would have been impossible to find. He was tireless, eager, alert, and so highly intelligent that after having seen him at work out in the paddocks on one occasion, she wouldn't have been at all surprised to learn that the dog was capable of mustering a complete flock on his own without requiring a single instruction.

For his part, Slade merely cast her a speaking glance. 'Since he's priceless as far as I'm concerned, both as a working dog and a sire, it would be a rather futile exercise trying to calculate his worth,' he drawled. 'Someone did try by making me an offer for him some months ago—an offer of five-and-a-half thousand, to be exact—but as you can tell, I knocked it back.'

'Without any later regrets?' she ventured to tease.

'Not a one!' His reply was categorical despite the smile that accompanied it.

By now, the pups on the ground had cursorily attempted to herd the sheep round the yard once more and were just in the process of wandering off to do a little investigating, and Taryn viewed their inquisitive meanderings with amusement.

'Won't you be getting them to do any more this morning?' she asked somewhat disappointedly.

'No, short daily lessons succeed far better than long ones that only tire, and often confuse them,' Slade advised as he began collecting his three charges. 'Besides, this was simply an introduction for them to freely moving sheep. They won't be put back in with them again until they've been taught all the necessary commands and they've learnt that they only work when they're directed to do so.'

Recovering the other two pups, Taryn added them

to the one still happily ensconced in her arms, and joined him in heading back to the kennels. 'Well, they seemed to acquit themselves quite reasonably, didn't they? You could even have another Ace amongst them.'

'Hopefully . . . since he's their sire.' The information was drily imparted as Slade deposited his pups in their yard.

'Oh, I didn't realise,' she both grimaced and flushed ruefully as she followed suit with her own three. On coming upright again, she looked about the other yards interestedly while Slade secured the gate. 'And their mother?'

'Cindy. The red and tan . . .'

'I know which one's Cindy,' she broke in to enlighten him, not a trifle smugly. Mainly, in retaliation for his last mockingly edged comment concerning the pups' sire. 'I feed them all, remember?'

'And you've memorised every one of their names already?' His brows peaked in half quizzical, half supposedly impressed raillery.

Trust him to ask that! she lamented inwardly, knowing that wasn't the case at all. Outwardly, she merely hunched a deprecating shoulder and parried, 'You said it was important I should call them all by name.'

'Mmm, except that doesn't exactly answer my question,' he was quick to observe.

Too quick for Taryn who sighed defeatedly and made a wry moue. He was nothing if not persistent! Or should she had said, relentless? 'Then if you must know, no I haven't managed to memorise all their names,' she divulged. 'I'm sorry, but I'm never quite sure if I've put the right name to the right dog with those over there.' Indicating an older litter that had already been assigned to individual kennels. A moment's hesitation, and she also confessed on a rueful note, 'Besides which, I somehow always seem to end up a name short for them as well.'

Unexpectedly, Slade laughed, his white teeth gleaming, his ebony-framed, smoky grey eyes crinkling engagingly at the corners. And Taryn's heart pounded raggedly against her ribs as a result. 'So why didn't you ask me to go through them all with you again?' he partly smiled, partly frowned. 'Considering there's thirty or so here at the moment it's not surprising you can't remember them all when we've only been over them together twice, or three times at the most.' His lips took on an oblique upward slant. 'To be quite truthful, you've already done better than I anticipated, so there's certainly no call for you to apologise.' Catching hold of her chin between thumb and forefinger, he tipped her face up to his, his gaze bantering as it connected with hers. 'Or am I so hard to work for that you feel you have to be on the defensive all the time?'

Actually, he was anything but difficult to work for, Taryn conceded. Perhaps it would have been easier if he had been! Because then she may not have been subjected to these wayward emotional responses that so confused and disconcerted her to such an extent— and especially now that his attitude towards her had altered so disturbingly.

'N-no,' she allowed self-consciously at length, struggling to regain control of the equilibrium that always seemed to desert her when she needed it most. 'I just didn't want to waste your time, or—or appear completely dense, I suppose.' And swallowing, on seeing those upward curves of his mouth beginning to broaden, desperately impelled a little tartness into her voice before his lazily emerging grin demolished the last of her small store of self-command altogether, continued hastily, 'While as for being on the defensive . . . well, why wouldn't I be? I've had more unfair and unverified allegations made against me by your family—apart from Jeff—than anyone else would reasonably expect to receive in a lifetime!'

'None of which *I've* added to since your arrival here, though.'

No, no he hadn't, and yet . . . And yet she was still inexplicably chary as to the reason why! Once again, maybe because his lack of opposition gave her less opportunities to combat the undeniable attraction he appeared to hold for her, she admitted in an unguarded flash of honesty. A supposition that understandably did little to overcome her present sense of disquiet.

'Possibly not, although your mother has definitely done her best to make up for your omission,' she consequently saw fit to charge. As much in an effort to keep the conversation from continuing on a personal level, as anything.

'Uh—uh!' Slade released her chin in order to wag a vetoing finger at her. 'You can't use that as an excuse, honey. Not when you're as aware as I am that she's unlikely to get the chance to do so again now that you're working solely for me.'

'An excuse!' she repeated with forced indignation. 'I don't need an excuse to be wary, I can assure you!'

'Hmm . . .' His ever-alert eyes scanned her slightly flushed features in leisurely speculation. 'But wary of what? Revealing more of your thoughts and feelings than you've persuaded yourself is wise?'

He was too close for comfort, both conjecturally and physically, and she half turned away with a restively agitated step. 'No! N-naturally not!' she all but squeaked, while at the same time berating herself for having so unthinkingly mouthed such a disastrous choice of word. '*If* I'm defensive, it's no doubt purely a carry-over from when I've needed to be. Pointing no fingers, of course!' She allowed herself the satisfaction of gibing, acidly explicit. Plus, hopefully disguising.

The grin she had previously been expecting with such consternation now made its appearance as Slade continued to eye her indolently, and Taryn knew she'd been right to try and discourage it, because her feelings immediately reacted in precisely the uncontrollable manner she had surmised they would. By setting her pulse racing capriciously, and constricting her throat so tightly that she found it almost impossible to breathe.

'W-e-ll,' he began in a lazy drawl, and her nerves tensing nearly as much as her throat in consequence, 'as they do happen to be the dogs I was planning to take down to the paddock this morning for more lessons, I guess it will be the perfect opportunity for correcting your little problem, won't it?'

Taryn couldn't nod rapidly enough, relieved beyond words that his attention had reverted to the dogs, regardless of the momentary suspicion that his suggestion may have carried a double meaning. Nevertheless, rather than ponder over it, she preferred to hurry across and collect the required animals, beginning to head for the paddock as soon as she had done so.

At least there, while Slade was conducting his training session, she would be free of any such perturbing confrontations, she reflected gratefully. And having thus taken care of the remainder of the morning, the afternoon would undoubtedly be likewise unexceptional because it had already been arranged for Burt Albright to accompany them while a thorough check was made of the property's grain-handling facilities in readiness for the coming season's harvest.

While tonight, her thoughts skipped onwards happily, she was going to a party with Jeff. He'd mentioned it to her only shortly after Slade had left the breakfast table that morning and she had accepted the idea readily. At the time, simply because it represented a chance to visit another property in the district, but now she was looking forward to it even more as a break from her employer's increasingly discomposing company!

'I didn't realise they would be coming too,' murmured Taryn in a somewhat dismayed aside to Jeff as they left the dining room that evening. She had only just discovered during dinner that both his brother and mother would also be attending the party that night, and although she was trying hard to conceal how diffident the disclosure had made her feel, it wasn't possible for her to disguise it altogether. The information had also come too late for her to back out of the arrangement, she realised despairingly.

Jeff merely shrugged impassively. 'But everyone always turns out when there's something on in the bush. Besides,' his shoulders lifted again, 'if I remember correctly Mother is Shirley's godmother, so since it is a birthday party, I suppose she would consider it her duty to go even if the rest of us didn't put in an appearance.'

'I see,' she acknowledged, grimacing to herself. She just wished he had thought to tell her that when he'd originally mentioned the matter. 'I guess we'll all be travelling together as well, then?'

'There wouldn't be much point in taking two vehicles when there's only the four of us,' he contended, sending her a curious look.

'No, of course not,' she concurred swiftly with a passably indifferent smile. She didn't want to arouse his suspicions to such a degree that he started questioning her about her misgivings. 'So I'll meet you down here in about,' she consulted her watch, 'another ten minutes, shall I?'

'Mmm, about that,' he acceded casually as they began going their separate ways. He, towards the sitting room, and Taryn upstairs to her bedroom.

Already dressed in the same black velvet skirt she had worn to the show dance and cabaret, but on this occasion teamed with a cap-sleeved and lightly beaded cross-over top of lilac jersey, she only needed to touch up her minimal make-up and collect her crocheted wrap and small evening purse, but even so she waited the full ten minutes before making her way down to the hall again—putting off the dreaded hour for as long as possible, she supposed with grimly wry humour—and found the other three just emerging from the sitting room.

'You're late!' promptly rebuked Mrs Douglas, looking down her aquiline nose at her. 'We've been waiting to leave for the past five minutes or more!'

'Well ... two, anyway,' amended Slade drily, and received a speaking glance from his parent for his interference.

'I—I'm sorry,' Taryn stammered, a placatory smile faltering on to her lips. The older woman's doubly critical demeanour since failing to have her dismissed wasn't precisely encouraging. 'I understood we wouldn't be leaving until eight.'

'Which time has now passed!' Mrs Douglas

snapped, haughtily indicating the grandfather clock nearby that showed the time as being a mere two minutes past the hour. The two minutes they had been standing there discussing the matter! judged Taryn pungently. 'In any case, in this house we leave when *I'm* ready to depart, not when some member of the staff finally decides it's time for us to do so!'

Taryn sucked in a resentful breath at the unwarranted accusation, but it was Jeff who stepped in to defend her. 'That's something of an exaggeration, isn't it, Mother? I mean, eight *was* the time decided upon during dinner, and it's not as if a minute or two either way matters, surely.'

'Yes, as it so happens, it does matter in my estimation!' came the unbending, frosty return. 'It's a matter of principle! Of not being expected to suffer the self-indulgent whims of the hired help! Not that it altogether surprises me, of course, that you should choose to disregard such considerations, Jefferson! After all, and to my utter disappointment, your own behaviour too often leaves much to be desired also, and particularly when you seem to go out of your way to purposely ignore my wishes!' With which biting stricture she whirled and, raising a heavily be-ringed hand to the collar of the fabulous white mink coat that was draped so cavalierly about her shoulders, swept majestically towards the front door.

In the momentary silence that followed, Taryn paused to wonder whether that reference to Jeff's ignoring his mother's wishes conversely implied that Slade was usually more amenable to them. As for example, where Ilona was concerned! Everything to date seemed to point that way, otherwise why would that girl continue visiting the Douglas homestead as regularly as she did? She had arrived on the scene at least another four times since Taryn's first day there, and to her knowledge Slade had even visited the Welbourne property on two other evenings, all of which appeared to indicate he wasn't as averse to the match as he sometimes gave the impression as being. Exactly as she had initially half surmised!

Strangely, she found it a rather dampening thought—probably because she, personally, had found Ilona to be totally unlikeable and as a result was appalled at the notion she might still be repaying Luke's debts when the other girl eventually did become Merringannee's new mistress, she decided— and wasn't at all sorry when Jeff interrupted her dispirited reverie.

'Don't let Mother's reprimands spoil your evening, little one,' he smiled encouragingly into her glum face as he dropped an arm about her shoulders in a friendly fashion and began ushering her in his mother's wake. He grinned boyishly. 'Her bark is really worse than her bite, you know.' Something Taryn found extremely difficult to believe! 'So just let it go in one ear and out the other. That's what I usually do.'

'Mainly because, in his case, there's nothing there to prevent anything from going straight through,' quipped Slade with a chafing look in his brother's direction as he moved up on Taryn's other side.

Jeff's eyes narrowed mock menacingly in retaliation, but it was Taryn who took it further by suggesting with dubious sweetness, 'You, of course, never experiencing any such problems ... because you always willingly fall in with your mother's wishes?' Her finely marked brows assumed a gently taunting arch.

'Oh, I don't know I'd say that exactly,' he demurred, and lowered his head nearer to hers before adding in a drily eloquent drawl, 'Otherwise it's extremely unlikely you would still be employed here, isn't it?'

He was referring to the earrings episode, naturally, and she averted her gaze, saved from admitting as much by a frowning insertion from Jeff.

'You mean, Mother's still opposed to your having hired Taryn because of what her brother did? I thought she'd more or less become resigned to that by now.'

'On occasion it would appear—not quite.' Slade's understatement was made on an ironic note, although it did at least enable Taryn to give a sigh of relief that he hadn't elaborated on what he suspected was their mother's main cause for opposition now. That could only have been embarrassing in the extreme.

Jeff shook his head in disbelief. 'That's a shame, and,' glancing down at Taryn sympathetically, 'I guess it can hardly make it pleasant for you either, knowing she's continuing to think that way.'

'You could say that.' she allowed somewhat absently as her thoughts suddenly turned inward. And because Mrs Douglas did evidently still dislike her so much, for whichever reason, wasn't there a distinct possibility that she could have informed the whole district that Taryn was the untrustworthy sister of the person who had stolen her son's wallet? Or if she hadn't already done so, might unkindly make it known at the party tonight while everyone was present, and especially if Ilona—who was sure to attend since Jeff had said everyone turned up for such events in the bush! she recalled in mounting dismay—was there to not only endorse the idea, but would undoubtedly be more than willing to voice a few spiteful barbs of her own!

More than ever now, she began to wish she had

declined to attend the party she had ironically been looking forward to all day. Just the thought of such a humiliating disclosure was sufficient to have her nerves shredding uncontrollably with an apprehension that, after she had reluctantly taken a seat in the station wagon waiting outside, was to increase with every mile that took them closer to their destination.

The Thorpe homestead, Taryn saw when they finally arrived, was perhaps smaller than the Douglas's, although certainly no less prosperous looking and, judging by the many well-lit rooms, together with the music and general sounds of merriment emanating therefrom, well able to cater for the large crowd of visitors the number of vehicles parked along the wide driveway indicated were already inside.

The fact that there obviously were so many present, however, only seemed to add to Taryn's tension, so much so that by the time she had mounted the steps leading on to the homestead's long, tiled porch she came to a sudden halt, her feet refusing to carry her any closer to the open front door before them as a totally demoralising picture flashed into her mind. It was an image of being mortifyingly cold-shouldered by every person there the minute she walked into the house due to them all having been informed of her brother's transgressions.

'Come on, Taryn, you're dragging the chain,' Jeff turned to joke on finding himself at the doorway with his mother only.

When there was no reply, nor movement immediately forthcoming, Slade who had been bringing up the rear, now came to a halt beside her.

'What's up, honey?' he probed intently on noting the tightness of not only her face, but her whole stance. 'You have an awfully strange look about you.'

'Strange? You mean, scared, don't you? Afraid of mixing with her betters, most likely!' Mrs Douglas put in patronisingly from the doorway. 'I told you she should never have been invited to accompany us.'

Whether he believed his mother's supposition or not, Taryn couldn't tell, but it did at least thankfully serve to break the trance-like alarm that had momentarily gripped her. Since she had never considered the possession of wealth as any criteria for deeming anyone better than another—in fact, if Mrs Douglas was an example, she would have said it had the completely opposite effect!—the charge that she was frightened of mixing with these people for that particular reason was just what she needed to have her angling her head defiantly and moving forward again.

'I'm sorry,' she apologised stiffly to Slade as he kept pace at her side. 'My mind must have been wandering for a moment. Although not . . .' she paused, her gaze unconsciously concentrating on his mother's impatiently waiting figure, 'because of any fear brought on by the thought of meeting any of my *supposed* betters, I can assure you!'

The quirk to his sensuous mouth abruptly became markedly apparent. 'I didn't suppose for one moment that it was,' he revealed in the driest of tones.

'Although it did at least succeed in getting her moving again, didn't it?' declared Mrs Douglas with obvious satisfaction—unbelievably, wryly amused satisfaction—as she continued on through the doorway.

Taryn could only stare after her in stunned amazement, finding it almost impossible to credit she had interpreted the older woman's subtle nuance correctly until Slade gave a soft laugh on seeing her dumbfounded expression.

'Mother has an—umm—whimsical sense of humour

at times,' he advised lazily. Halting, his gaze assumed
a faintly ironic cast. 'She's not exactly lacking in
perception either.'

'You're saying, she purposely made that remark
because she *knew* what my reaction would be?' she
gasped incredulously.

'As like as not,' he shrugged.

'I told you her bark was worse than her bite, didn't
I?' This from Jeff as they reached him and together
followed Mrs Douglas into the homestead's carpeted
entrance hall.

'But—but . . .' She stammered helplessly to a stop,
shaking her head in disbelief. But not where she was
concerned! she had wanted to disclaim, only it did
seem a little inappropriate to do so at a time when
that had apparently just been disproved.

However, it did give rise to a host of hitherto
unconsidered possibilities, even though there was no
opportunity for her to deliberate over them because
their arrival had now been noted and a return of the
tension that had attacked her so disconcertingly before
immediately put anything else out of her mind as she
prepared to meet—and gauge the response—of the
young brunette who emerged from a noisily filled
room on the left of the hall to greet them.

A few minutes later, and their introduction
completed, Taryn was gratefully able to relax a little
more. From her open and friendly reaction it had been
evident that Shirley Thorpe, at least, either knew
nothing of the affair concerning Luke, or if she did,
was charitably prepared not to bracket his sister along
with him, and as a result it allowed Taryn to
participate in their ensuing entry into the spacious
room where most of the dancing was taking place in a
considerably easier state of mind.

Here, too, she was even more thankful to discover, those people Jeff did permit her to meet before whisking her away to join the enthusiastically, or desultorily—as the mood took them—moving dancers, had also been most pleasant. Apart from one exception, that was.

Unfortunately, one of the first persons they had happened to come across had been a magnificently attired Ilona Welbourne whose as good as non-existent acknowledgment of Taryn's reluctantly proferred greeting had promptly been followed by the purposely patronising and belittling observation to Mrs Douglas as that woman took a seat beside the lemon-chiffon-and-lace arrayed girl on a tapestry covered sofa, 'You know, Bernadette, you really will have to give your newest employee the benefit of your experience regarding clothes if she intends to continue tagging along with you to functions such as this. It's obvious she needs someone's assistance . . . or don't tell me,' she paused to utter a derisively amused laugh, her brown eyes, sardonically enquiring, flicking upwards to Taryn, 'that the reason you're wearing that same shabby skirt you wore to the show cabaret is because you don't possess anything more suitable . . . or better?'

An involuntary flush had mounted Taryn's cheeks almost immediately. Not because she considered her skirt was shabby—as she had only ever worn it on a few occasions, how could it have been?—or even in surprise at the other girl having paid her enough attention at the cabaret to note what she had been wearing, but because the remark had been voiced deliberately loud enough for everyone within ten foot of them to have heard.

'It's neither, actually,' she had forced herself to

smile back, defensively mocking. 'Since I wasn't anticipating doing much socialising while employed at Merringannee, it's the *only* one I have with me ... suitable or otherwise.'

'And I think she looks delightful in it,' had interposed Jeff supportively. His brother merely listening in impassive silence, Taryn noted.

'Mmm, but then I've no doubt you'd feel very ungallant if you didn't say as much,' Ilona had promptly retorted with a smile that was evidently supposed, even if it wasn't quite successful, to cover the acid in her words.

'Uh-uh!' Jeff had squashed that notion with a quick shake of his head, a touch of mockery in his glance as it rested on the other girl. 'There's no need to be gallant just for the sake of it where Taryn's concerned because she always looks good whatever she's wearing. She's one of the fortunate few who don't require expensive and elaborate finery in order to enhance *their* appearance,' he stressed sardonically.

Actually, Taryn didn't think that Ilona did either, because the older woman's features were really quite lovely. At least they were when they weren't taking on such a vengeful mien in response to that purposely taunting emphasis as they were now, she qualified ruefully.

'Then you evidently have as little conception regarding acceptable standards of dress as she does!' Ilona had snapped, obviously feeling slighted. 'And if you bothered to look around you, you could see for yourself that I'm right in saying something like *that* doubtlessly bargain basement outfit,' with a contemptuous look in Taryn's direction, 'is totally out of place here!'

'Oh, I don't know about that,' had interjected Slade

unexpectedly, drily, his eyes scanning the occupants of the room cursorily. 'I notice Zoë Burgess is still on her handkerchief headband and see-through muslin kick.'

'Y-yes—well—everyone knows Zoë likes to think of herself as something of an eccentric,' Ilona had excused, though the glance that had accompanied it hadn't offered any excuse for his interference. 'In any case, she's wealthy enough to get away with it. It's not as if she doesn't *know* how to dress correctly if it suits her.'

Taryn's lips had twisted obliquely at that. In other words, it was yet again another instance of there being one set of rules for the rich and another for the poor!

'Except that Zoë Burgess's taste in clothes has always been atrocious, even when she pays a fortune for them.' It was Mrs Douglas who, even more unexpectedly, had joined the conversation with a disparaging snort this time.

'You've never said a truer word!' Jeff had chortled. Then, catching Taryn around the waist, 'Nevertheless, since I didn't come here to discuss clothes of any description, if you'll excuse us I think we'll join in with the dancing while I still have the chance to partner Taryn . . . because I don't doubt there's plenty of other males here who won't give a damn as to what she's wearing either!' With which parting shot aimed at Ilona they had finally taken their leave.

Now, as they continued moving casually to the beat of a current disco tune, Taryn found herself mulling over the conversation thoughtfully. Of course Ilona's remarks had been precisely what she'd come to expect from the Douglas's condescending neighbour. On those occasions when she had visited Merringannee, and Taryn had been unable to avoid her completely, there had always been some derisive, or just plain corrosive, comments to suffer, but as far as she could recall, tonight was the first time Mrs Douglas hadn't either directly or tacitly supported everything Ilona said.

Admittedly, the older woman's difference of opinion a short time ago had merely been with regard to an acquaintance's style of raiment—which didn't altogether surprise Taryn in view of the fact that Mrs Douglas's own wardrobe consisted of nothing but the most becomingly tasteful apparel—but it was still a departure from what had been the norm to date and she couldn't help pondering what had caused the breach in their solidarity.

Or perhaps it wasn't a breach at all, she went on to amend wryly a few unproductive minutes later, but simply a case of Mrs Douglas expressing their actual unanimous viewpoint because by having been forced to defend the unknown Zoë, it had then been out of the question for Ilona to voice her true opinion on the subject. Which seemed a far more likely circumstance, and having arrived at that conclusion Taryn dismissed the matter from her mind and determinedly set about enjoying the remainder of the evening.

CHAPTER SIX

WHEN it was served a few hours later, supper was a sumptuous buffet affair, complete with a magnificently iced and decorated birthday cake adorned with eighteen candles that required two attempts from a flushed and laughing Shirley to blow them all out. The accompanying champagne toasts, Taryn found, made her feel more carefree than she had done for some considerable time as they mixed with the other wine she had earlier been plied with between dances.

It was a blithe, lighthearted sensation that was still with her when the music resumed and everyone gradually began dancing again afterwards, and it enabled her to accept Slade's offer to dance with an insouciance she very much doubted she could have managed otherwise. As it happened, this was the first occasion he had approached her, and although she certainly hadn't lacked for partners previously that hadn't prevented her from being all too aware of the other females he had chosen to partner—Ilona most frequently, she had observed with a grimace—and she had spent a large proportion of her time wondering whether he intended rectifying the position or not—and the rest debating with herself as to whether she actually *wanted* him to or not!

On the one hand she had been half wishing he would—after all, he was an undeniably attractive man—but on the other, she had worried that where she was concerned he could just prove to be a little too attractive, particularly when keeping in mind the events of the night before! Now, it appeared, she was about to discover which choice would have been the correct one.

'Well, you seem to have quite taken the young men of the district by storm,' Slade drawled whimsically as they made their way around the room to a soft, slow tune. Not even the youngest of those present had felt like anything more lively so soon after such an impressive supper. 'It's been impossible to get anywhere near you.'

'I didn't notice you even trying,' Taryn glanced upwards through thickly curling lashes to charge chaffingly. 'From what I saw, you were—umm—more than content lavishing your attention upon someone else entirely.'

'Lavishing?' He disputed the description with an amused laugh. 'Hardly that, honey. Besides,' his grey eyes connected with hers tauntingly, 'I would have thought you were far too occupied yourself to have noticed what I happened to be doing.'

'I was just trying to be a good employee and keep track of my boss's whereabouts,' she quipped glibly, shrugging.

'So you could take the necessary steps to ensure you continued keeping any contact between us to the minimum . . . the same as you've been doing all day?'

'I didn't think you'd realised,' she sparkled provokingly. Then promptly berated herself for allowing the wine she had consumed to do her talking for her. It was all very well experiencing such an uncustomary nonchalance in his presence, but not to the extent of sounding even mildly flirtatious!

Slade pulled her closer to his muscular form, the warmth of his hand against her back penetrating the material of her top and sending a peculiarly shivery feeling trickling down her spine. 'There's quite a few things I realise about you, Taryn Rodgers. Not the least of which is that you'd rather deny than admit that we're neither as averse to the other as you would like to pretend,' he bent his head to murmur close to her ear.

Taryn jerked her head away rapidly, conscious all of a sudden that they had somehow progressed from the main dancing area to a connecting, but much more dimly lit—and unoccupied—smaller room. She moistened her lips nervously. 'Only according to you,' she asserted as positively as possible.

'You reckon?' he drawled. 'How about we put it to the test, then, hmm?'

'There's nothing to test!' she all but croaked in her haste to protest, and ineffectually attempted to pull out of his arms.

Slade didn't even bother to reply, he simply used one arm to keep her captive while the other slid between the silky strands of her brightly coloured hair in order to immobilise her head, and his lips preceeded to slant across hers in a hard, demanding kiss that consummately swept aside her defences even as she tried to deny the pleasure his mouth was creating, and which left her shaking when he at last raised his head.

Catching her face between his hands now, his thumbs stroking her jawline tantalisingly, he tipped her head upwards so she couldn't evade his unusually dark gaze. 'So what do *you* call that chemistry that flares between us ... indifference?' he mocked huskily.

Taryn moved her head helplessly, still in the throes of some emotion she could neither explain nor control. 'I—I'm ... oh, please,' she begged incoherently.

'Please what, Taryn?' he probed insistently, his mouth brushing lightly, devastatingly, over hers. 'Please stop . . . or please continue?'

She swallowed heavily, her lavender eyes surveying his intent features searchingly, her hands tentatively beginning to creep upward towards his neck as if of their own volition. 'Oh, please continue,' she groaned on a partly defeated, partly fervent note as her desire to resist abruptly crumbled completely.

This time the lips that parted hers were persuasively caressing and as her response came spontaneously her curving shape arched invitingly against the hard masculinity of his, her fingers tangling within the dark hair at the back of his head, and she abandoned herself to the wild enjoyment of the moment. He had the ability to destroy her defences like no other man she had ever met before, and when her incredibly heightened senses were clamouring so overpoweringly for her to reciprocate, it seemed useless to pretend otherwise.

Relinquishing her lips momentarily, Slade's mouth sought the throbbing cord at the side of her arched throat, his hands simultaneously sliding slowly, sensuously, down her back to her hips, pressing her closer to his sinewed length, and then just as leisurely seeking the slender contours of her waist before moving upwards again to cup her swelling breasts as his lips masterfully claimed her once more.

A liquid fire engulfed Taryn, sending uncontrollable tides of passion and longing searing through her to the extremity of every limb. He was arousing feelings she had never imagined she would ever experience, and as his hands continued their caressing exploration she couldn't restrain the quiver of wanton ecstasy that overtook her.

Then, the sound of approaching voices abruptly assailed her ears, reminding her of their whereabouts, and causing her to give a muffled gasp as she self-consciously sought to break free of Slade's embrace. Refusing to release her immediately, however, he kept her pinned close to his side with an arm around her shoulders, his free hand tilting her rosily illuminated face up to his as he possessed her soft mouth in one last intoxicating kiss.

'I only wish to God we were somewhere more private,' he sighed deeply against her still-parted lips as he lifted his head with obvious reluctance.

And to Taryn's unbounded embarrassment and consternation that was exactly the betraying position they were in when Mrs Douglas and Ilona, of all people, entered the room. Stiffening apprehensively, she promptly made to put more distance between herself and Slade, but the decided tightening of his arm about her shoulders effectively forestalled any such move. Which evidently didn't go unnoticed by the younger of the women facing them.

'There! I told you I knew what she was up to the minute I saw them come in here! She even looks as guilty as hell!' Ilona raged infuriatedly to Mrs Douglas. 'The same as I warned you the very first day she arrived at Merringannee that Slade was her only reason for working there!' She swung her irate gaze on to Taryn. 'It's more than obvious she's no different from her brother! Neither of them can keep their thieving hands off someone else's property, but this time she's gone too far, and she needn't think I'm going to obligingly permit her to steal something of mine!'

'And just what might that be ... this so-called property of yours?' Slade enquired in a low, but unmistakably cold tone.

Briefly, Ilona stared at him almost open-mouthed, and then twin spots of brilliant colour invaded her cheeks. 'I—why—you, of course,' she stammered in nothing like her normal arrogantly assured manner. 'I mean, you know very well we have—have an understanding ...'

'Do we?' he countered with a slightly mocking uplift of one brow that relieved his expression of some of its coolness, but not his voice. 'I didn't realise.'

'Oh, don't give me that!' Ilona burst out furiously, recovering somewhat. 'It's been intended that we should marry for some months now ... as everyone, including yourself, is well aware!'

'So you keep saying, but unfortunately *I* don't happen to recall ever agreeing to any such arrangement!'

'W-well, maybe not in so many words,' Ilona was prepared—or forced—to concede, though with evident reluctance, 'but until this—this brazenly designing trollop came long,' a virulent sneer was aimed at Taryn which had the younger woman sucking in an indignant breath, 'you certainly seemed to accept the idea willingly enough, so I rather think it's a little late for you to be claiming otherwise now just because *she's* proving to be so shamelessly accommodating!' She halted, her demeanour altering to one of gloating. 'And if that wasn't the case, as you're trying to infer, then why else have you been such a frequent visitor to my home? Explain your way out of that, then ... *if* you can!'

Slade flexed an indifferent shoulder. 'In view of the fact that your brother and I have been mates ever since I can remember, and since I usually spend by far the greatest proportion of my time in discussion with him, I would have thought the reason was all too obvious!' he elucidated so unsparingly that, despite her dislike of the other girl, Taryn felt sorry for her. If anyone ever spoke to her like that she just knew she would die of embarrassment.

Judging by the waves of hot colour that surged into Ilona's pale cheeks, it became apparent her ego had just suffered a severe blow too, although that still didn't prevent her from persevering tenaciously, 'And the times I visited Merringannee when you didn't hesitate to stop whatever you were doing in order to be with me?'

'Uh-uh, not exactly to be with you,' he contradicted with a slow but definite shake of his head. 'More to be hospitable because I knew it was expected ... hoped,' an implicit look was directed towards his parent, 'of me.'

After such a humiliating set-down anyone else would have preferred not to pursue the matter—at least, not right then and there in public—Taryn was sure, but not so Ilona, for in spite of the colour staining her cheeks deepening noticeably, it seemed she still refused to even acknowledge the possibility of defeat.

'Like hell it was to be hospitable!' she retorted, her brown eyes flashing fiercely. 'You may have been able to convince *her* of that,' jeeringly, 'but you needn't think I'm going to be so obligingly gullible just because she's shown herself willing to climb into bed with you—as she's undoubtedly done with countless others before!—because I happen to know better! As your own mother can confirm, even if you're loath to!' She looked to the, until now, silent woman beside her for support.

Suspecting she already knew precisely how Mrs Douglas would view the matter, and resenting Ilona's derogatory remarks anyway. Taryn decided to put in a few words of her own, but as she opened her mouth to begin Slade's fingers tightened their grasp on her shoulder warningly and surprise had her hesitating so that it was eventually his mother who spoke first after all.

'Yes, well, whether I can or not, I'm more inclined to feel this is neither the time nor the place to be indulging in any such discussion, Ilona.' The faintly reproving contention was voiced briskly, to both the younger women's evident astonishment—although for entirely differing reasons. The only one the comment didn't appear to have caught offguard was Slade, Taryn noticed, and then supposed that it really was only to be expected since who else would be likely to know his parent's probable reactions better? It also explained the reason behind that warning grip of his, for which she was now extremely thankful. 'I've always believed family affairs, and differences, should be settled within the privacy of the home, not in public where anyone might possibly overhear, and certainly not while as a guest in someone else's home!' she concluded meaningfully.

'I'll subscribe to that!' seconded Slade on a hard note.

'Oh, yes, no doubt you would!' Ilona rounded on him in caustic fury. 'In view of your contemptible behaviour towards me tonight I'm not surprised you're embarrassed at the thought of it becoming common gossip!' She turned to Mrs Douglas, whose apparent defection obviously wasn't to be permitted to escape unremarked either. 'However, I am surprised, not to say overwhelmingly disappointed, that you can see fit to accept such appalling conduct without one word of denunciation, Bernadette! And especially when you're fully aware that everything I've said has been nothing but the absolute truth!'

Unquestionably nettled at being taken to task in such a fashion, particularly in front of an employee, Mrs Douglas drew herself up to her full, commanding height and fixed the blonde-headed girl with an imperious stare. 'Not, according to my son, apparently!' she retaliated pungently. 'While as for your comments regarding behaviour . . .' she drew in a deeply disapproving breath, 'I'm afraid I haven't exactly found yours laudable this evening, Ilona, because this is definitely not the scene I envisaged having thrust upon me when you suggested I should accompany you in here, nor the type I'm accustomed to being embroiled in in public, I'm thankful to say.' Pausing she made an obvious effort to inject a little more warmth into her tone. 'So now might I suggest that the two of us return to the sitting room and leave any further deliberations on the subject for some more suitable time and venue?'

'You mean, you're not even going to say anything to *her*?' Ilona couldn't refrain from demanding incredulously as she flung out a wildly indicating hand.

Mrs Douglas executed an imperceptible shrug. 'Under the circumstances, I think it would be rather difficult to admonish total silence, don't you?' she replied with a touch of dryness as she began making for the doorway.

'But—but—what about . . .' Ilona started to expostulate, then came to a halt with an acrimonious thinning of her lips on seeing her only possible supporter disappearing into the next room. Recognising, if not quite accepting, temporary defeat at least, she promptly spun on her own heel and prepared to follow the older woman, but not without one last malicious parting shot for Taryn.

'Although he may stoop to bed you, I can assure you he won't stoop to wed you, if that's what you're angling for! Not someone with your inferior and unsavoury background!' she half laughed, half jeered as she too took her leave.

As neither consideration had actually entered Taryn's mind, the spiteful prediction didn't really worry her unduly, but the thought that Slade may perhaps have been labouring under the same misconception as his blonde neighbour was something else again. It had her cringing inwardly and hastily, self-consciously, attempting to correct any such inaccuracy.

'I—er—had no thoughts along those lines, anyway,' she disclaimed awkwardly, her head downbent, and in an effort to divert his attention went on hurriedly. 'I was surprised at what your mother had to say, though. I was all prepared for her to support Ilona to the hilt.'

'So I gathered,' he smiled wryly. 'Although the one who really should have known better was Ilona. Because as Mother said, she's never been one to tolerate scenes of any kind in public, while as for anyone criticising one of her family ...' his lips twitched evocatively, 'well, no matter how much she may do so herself, woe betide any outsider who dares to do the same—as Ilona should have been aware.'

Looking up slightly, Taryn's eyes widened expressively. 'I didn't think she *did* consider Ilona an outsider. I mean, I thought it was all arranged that you—that you and she ...' Reddening, she stammered to a halt, averting her gaze again. Then, sucking in a steadying breath she tried once more. 'Well, Ilona was also obviously under the impression that the two of you were to marry,' she concluded on a rather more accusing note than she intended in her effort to sound indifferent.

'Apparently,' he conceded with a whimsical movement of his head. 'Although I somehow doubt she is any more.'

'Your mother either?'

'Unless I miss my guess, I suspect she finally resigned herself to the inevitable the minute Ilona somewhat imprudently began claiming I was her property. A very provoking, not to say presumptuous, judgment on her part, that.'

Because he had never intended to marry Ilona, or because he just never intended to marry . . . period? Taryn found herself speculating with a vague unexplainable feeling of dullness.

'So it would appear you've done me quite a favour, wouldn't it?'

The drawling supposition brought her out of her reverie with a start as, for some indefinable reason, or maybe due to a particular subtlety she thought she detected in his tone, it suddenly reminded her of her initial suspicions regarding his decision to employ her.

'For—for having conveniently fallen in with your plans to destroy theirs?' she queried tightly.

Briefly, Slade's grey eyes flickered, but whether in expectation or with some other emotion she couldn't quite decide, and then they were concentrating steadily again on her stiffly held features. 'For being so damned irresistible, more like,' he amended in something of a rueful growl as he swiftly, competently, bent and branded her unsuspecting lips with his own once more.

But the time he released them again, Taryn was too occupied in attempting to restore some control over the turbulent emotions he always seemed able to arouse within her so effortlessly to even think of anything else, let alone try to analyse faint intonations she may only have imagined anyway. Not that it would have done her much good even if she had, she realised, because scant seconds later Jeff appeared in the doorway and then any further deliberations were completely out of the question.

'There you are!' he exclaimed cheerily on catching sight of her. 'I've been looking everywhere for you. You promised me another dance after supper, remember?' Halting, he cast his brother a bantering glance. 'Or would that be classified as intruding?'

'No, of course not.' It was Taryn who quickly made the denial as she slipped out from beneath the arm that had still been resting across her shoulders, and moved forward. Not only did she not want to give Slade the impression that she considered she had any claim on his attention, but she also felt the need to be free of his disturbing company for a while in order to sort out her own feelings—and the direction in which they were going! 'I was just about to come and look for you, actually,' she added, albeit not altogether truthfully, on reaching Jeff and linking her arm with his.

'We'll see you later, then,' he turned to advise Slade with a grin as he began escorting her from the room.

'Uh-huh,' came the drily laconic affirmation as Slade too started for the door, his accompanying expression sending a shiver of part excitement, part apprehension down Taryn's spine on involuntarily looking back and seeing it. Evidently she had caught his interest, but right at the moment she couldn't make up her mind whether that was good or bad!

*

In the weeks that followed, and as spring inevitably gave way to the extreme heat of summer—although the southern State of Victoria wasn't generally regarded as having high temperatures, the sandy inland plains of the Mallee district were a definite exception—Taryn found it impossible to continue denying the undoubted magnetism she felt towards her attractive boss, and once she had finally admitted it did actually exist, it didn't require very much soul-searching on her part to discover why. She had gradually, but irrevocably, fallen in love with him! And probably had been, if the truth was known, ever since their initial meeting when he had made such an unaccountable impact on her at first glance, notwithstanding his subsequently less than affable manner on occasion!

For a while the realisation had caused her a certain amount of disquiet, but as it became progressively obvious that Slade wasn't exactly averse to her either—as well as perhaps most importantly of all, Ilona was now conspicuous only by her absence—she was eventually able to relax her previously guarded attitude in his company and allow her naturally warm nature to shine through knowing, or at least strongly suspecting, that her feelings weren't entirely un-reciprocated.

As far as she was concerned there wasn't a cloud on her horizon, and not even Mrs Douglas's niggling comments—admittedly, though completely in-explicably, noticeably less in number and intensity these days—were sufficient to disturb her carefree sense of happiness, or have her returning to the show circuit as her brother Luke tried to persuade her to do when he put in an astonishing sneak appearance at the property late one afternoon.

At the time Taryn was feeding the dogs while

simultaneously admiring another of the magnificent red and gold sunsets for which the area was renowned, and although she started a little when a male figure abruptly, noiselessly, loomed out of the shadows close by it was more in mild surprise than alarm as she presumed it was Burt taking a short cut through to his own quarters. It wasn't until he spoke that she recognised just who it was and then her expression did register incredulity, together with a certain degree of apprehension.

'Luke?' The confirmation-seeking gasp was forced from her involuntarily as if she still couldn't quite bring herself to believe she had heard correctly. Her eyes flicked over the surrounding area with a nervous swiftness. 'Where did you come from, and what on earth are you doing here, anyway? You must know you're not exactly on the family welcome list here at the moment!'

'Which is why I left the bike about a mile away and covered the rest on foot, dodging from tree to tree so I wouldn't be seen,' he relayed on an irritated note at having been put to such trouble. 'As for why I'm here . . .' he shrugged, looking a trifle uncomfortable, 'well, I only heard a couple of days ago from the folks that you'd stayed behind here, and . . .'

'You mean, it's been all this time until you actually returned?' she broke in, slightly reproving, as the import of his words hit her.

He did at least have the grace to look abashed, however, she noted. 'Yeah, well, time just kind of got away from me a bit, I guess,' he tried to justify. Adding in a voice strengthening with a little resentment, 'But at least as soon as I found out this is where you were I came to see how you were making out!'

'Then, thank you.' She gave a conciliatory half smile before her forehead began to furrow quizzically. 'Although I'm not sure just why you apparently thought it was necessary.'

'Because of what happened at the show in Jinda Jinda, of course,' he divulged with a return of a somewhat sheepish look. 'After all, I did help myself to a fair sum of Douglas's money—not that he couldn't afford it, mind!' he inserted blusteringly, 'but at the same time, if the last expression I saw on his face was any indication, I sincerely doubt he was in the mood to be acquiescing to some sudden and supposed request for employment by any relation of mine, no matter what far-fetched story you spun for Mum and Dad's benefit!' Pausing, his eyes narrowed as he watched her intently. 'So just why are you here, Taryn? Because he threatened to lay charges against me if the money wasn't repaid . . . or is it payment in another form he's been demanding?'

'No!' Her vehement denial was unequivocal even though she wasn't surprised that his former assumption should have been so near the truth. Knowing more of what had occurred, it was only logical that he wouldn't accept her story as unsuspectingly as their parents had done, and especially when he had always been extremely quick-witted anyway. 'As a matter of fact, he didn't do either,' she went on to explain. 'Oh, you're right of course in supposing that's the reason I'm here, but it was all my idea, believe me, because I *offered* to repay the money.'

'And he agreed to employ you just to make it easier for you to do so?' sceptically.

'Well, no, not exactly, because once again it was my suggestion that he should employ me. At first he found the idea somewhat ironic too.'

'So what made him change his mind?'

'He figured it was the only way to ensure I wouldn't skip town the minute his back was turned, as he was of the opinion I probably would do if I was employed by someone else,' she revealed drily.

'He's not a very good judge of character, is he?' His lips curled scornfully.

'Considering the prevailing circumstances at the time, perhaps it wasn't so surprising,' she shrugged deprecatingly. Halting, something of a smile pulled at the edges of her mouth. 'I suspect he's revised his opinion now, though.'

Luke glanced at her contemplatively, then hunched a wiry shoulder in a dismissive movement as he pushed a hand into the back pocket of his jeans. 'Well, whether he has or not isn't important now, because you don't have to continue working here any more. You can pay him off with this and be done with the whole lot of them,' he advised, bringing forth a wad of fifty dollar notes which he held out to her.

Taken aback, Taryn merely stared at the bundle in his hand without making any move to accept it, her thoughts starting to race. If she did repay Slade there would be no reason for her to remain at Merringannee Bluff, and right at present that notion had no appeal whatsoever. Also, she was sure her parents could find far better uses to put such an obviously sizeable amount to. Then, of course, there was also the worrying thought to be considered as to just how Luke had come by the money in the first place, and it was this last concern that occupied her most of all.

'Oh, Luke, not again!' she partly despaired, partly admonished. 'Didn't your close shave last time teach you anything? You can't expect to keep getting away with these schemes, for want of a better word, of yours, you know. You're going to get caught some time and then there'll be nothing anyone can do to cover for you.'

'Except that this,' waving the money in front of her, 'didn't happen to come from any so-called scheme,' he retorted touchily. 'As it so happens, I won it fair and square on the races.'

'What races?' she probed, not altogether convinced.

'The gallops in Melbourne, if you must know.'

'You mean, that's why you've been away so long? You went all the way down to Melbourne?' she gasped.

'Why not?' he countered, sounding more than a little put out. 'I felt like a taste of city life, and it sure didn't seem wise to hang around too close to Jinda Jinda after what happened. Who knew what uproar Douglas was likely to create? Nor can I say it ever occurred to me that you'd go so far as to offer to make restitution.' He averted his gaze slightly, his tone somewhat less belligerent when he continued. 'But thanks all the same. I do appreciate it, even if it doesn't sound like it.' Inhaling swiftly, his attitude changed to one of urgency. 'And that's precisely why I want you to take this money now. Directly the folks told me where you were working I suspected something of the sort may have happened, and so I came straight back here with it in order to bail you out of this place.'

'Yes, well, that really was very thoughtful of you, and I am grateful, but . . .'

'It was all won on the square, honest!' he broke in to reassure insistently.

'I believe you,' she averred, trying to set his mind at rest. 'It's just that I'm inclined to think Mum and Dad have a greater need for some finance at the moment than I have, and—and especially since, to be quite truthful, I'm rather enjoying working here.' With a self-conscious flush she couldn't control.

On seeing it, Luke's originally surprised look promptly turned to one of sardonic gibing. 'Working here . . . or for *him*?'

Taryn half shrugged diffidently. 'I—I could have had worse for a boss.'

'In other words, you've flipped over the feller!' he deduced, but in something of a jeering rasp.

'And if I have?' she flared defiantly, taking exception to his tone.

'And if you have?' he repeated increduously, slapping an exasperated hand against his thigh. 'Good God, Taryn, are you out of your mind? Even if he is paying you some attention—and why wouldn't he when there's someone on hand with your looks?—you can't honestly believe anything permanent is ever likely to come of it! Men like him only marry their own kind—long-time, wealthy members of the Establishment—and usually in order to increase their holdings,' derisively. 'People with our type of background may rate an affair or two, but that's all it will be, you can take my word for it, and you'll be the one who gets hurt if you're tempted to think otherwise!'

Not that she had even reached the stage of looking that far into the future, but . . . 'And just where did you get all this knowledge as to what Slade's *kind* supposedly do and why?' she questioned on a slightly rankled note.

He shook his head impatiently. 'Oh, come off it, Taryn, you can't be that naïve! You know damned well money always marries money, and the formula's

not about to change just because you've come along!'
Breaking off suddenly, he expelled a long breath, his
manner softening sympathetically. 'I'm sorry, I know
you probably think it's none of my business, and that
I'm simply being prejudiced, but really, I don't want
to see my only sister hurt, that's all.' His blue eyes
sought hers coaxingly. 'Are you positive you couldn't
merely pay him back the money and then leave?'

Taryn smiled at him fondly. He was only trying to
protect her, when all was said and done. 'Mmm, I'm
positive,' she murmured softly, reaching out to clasp
his hand.

Luke returned the pressure comfortingly. 'You
honestly don't want any of this, then?' Lifting the
notes into view once more.

'No—thank you. I think I'd like to remain here a
while longer, all the same.'

'You're really that crazy about the guy?' he probed,
ruefully incredulous, as he replaced the money in his
pocket with evident reluctance.

Not trusting herself to speak, she nodded, shyly.

'Well, I guess that just about settles it, then, doesn't
it?' he sighed resignedly. Then, in a decidedly firmer
tone, 'But you take it careful, anyway, huh?'

'Don't worry, I will,' she promised.

'You'd better,' he mock threatened, giving her
fingers another brotherly squeeze before releasing
them. 'But if things don't turn out as you'd like, just
drop us a line care of the local post office—Mum said
you knew their itinerary—and I'll have you out of here
before you know it . . . even if I have to sell the bike to
raise the cash to do it.'

Aware just what a sacrifice he was offering, Taryn
hugged him gratefully. 'In the meantime, though, if I
don't finish feeding these soon . . .' with a grudging,

but expressive glance towards the dogs who had begun to punctuate the stillness of the evening with an increasing number of barks to remind her they were still waiting, 'I'm afraid someone might be down to investigate the noise, and . . .'

'As I'm not exactly a welcome guest, my presence undoubtedly wouldn't be appreciated,' Luke finished for her. Followed by a shrugged, 'And since I've said all I came to say, I guess I'd better be making tracks, anyhow. You just remember what I told you, though . . . all right?' The reminder was made as he began taking his leave.

'Okay,' she agreed with a fond smile. 'And you give my love to Mum and Dad.'

'Will do,' he nodded and, raising his hand in a brief salute, disappeared among the shadows again as suddenly and silently as he had arrived.

CHAPTER SEVEN

IF thoughts of marriage hadn't entered Taryn's mind before her brother's visit, they did afterwards as a result of what he had said, but although his contentions did cause her some moments of deep, and not always uplifting, deliberation on occasion, in the main she refused to allow them to disturb her overmuch.

For the time being she was more than prepared, not to say content, to have her relationship with Slade continue in precisely the same pleasant and stimulating manner as it had been doing before Luke's appearance, and so when he invited her to accompany him to the Agricultural Field Day to be held at Tantallon, a town some one hundred miles distant—it would be the last probably before their lives were filled with the approaching grain harvest—she accepted with a delighted alacrity. Just the idea of spending a whole day away from the property alone with him—well, alone in the sense they were the only two from Merringannee going, she had qualified with a wry chuckle—was sufficient to have her spirits bubbling with joy.

When the day duly arrived, of necessity Taryn arose while it was still dark. Slade intended taking fifteen dogs of assorted ages with them and it would take time to get them all loaded into their specially constructed, air-conditioned trailer, have a quick cup of coffee and a bite to eat for breakfast themselves, and still be away by five.

That they accomplished it so effortlessly was due in no small part to the fact that they did, indeed, seem to work well as a team, she mused happily on taking her seat in the front of the station wagon. As was further proved when Slade brought them to a halt at the boundary grid before emerging on to the road that led to the highway and turned to her with a look of wry disbelief crossing his face.

'I know they say there's a first time for everything, but never did I think to see the day when I'd forget the dogs' registration papers,' he disclosed in an expressive drawl. His ebony-framed gaze settled on her softly contoured mouth, 'I must have my mind on other things.'

Taryn tut-tutted teasingly even as her heart swelled in response. 'Then it's just as well *I* did remember them, isn't it?' She pointed to the glove box, not a little smugly. 'All present and correct, boss.'

With a grin he reached across and rumpled her red-gold hair in retribution, but his ensuing words weren't retaliatory at all, they were approving, and therefore wholly satisfying to his companion. 'You really did turn out to be a great little offsider, didn't you?' he commended.

'I do my best to please,' she quipped in an effort to disguise her unbelievably receptive emotions.

'And succeed perhaps too well at times,' he owned on a deepening note, then with a somewhat crooked tilt to his shapely mouth returned his attention to the vehicle and shortly had it in motion once more.

More conscious than she would have believed possible of a feeling of utter contentment, Taryn leant back in her seat to idly watch the scenery flash past them. Although most of the spring flowers had disappeared now, there were enough of the hardier specimens still in evidence to attract her notice—blue dampiera, golden everlasting daisies, scarlet coral pea, and orange and brown spotted emu bush—and as they were travelling in an easterly direction she also found it interesting to watch the whole aspect of the countryside change from open plain to denser woodland.

However, as this was the type of Victorian scenery she was more used to viewing while travelling with her parents her interest soon began to wane and she fell to pondering about the dogs in the trailer behind them instead. Three of the younger ones were from that very same litter she had first taken down to the sheep yard with Slade to gauge their reaction, and she knew they were the ones she would miss most of all if they were sold. She had come to think of them as being hers and was as doleful at the thought of losing them as if they had been. In fact, she reflected ruefully, she hated to see just about any of them leave.

'Why so pensive?' Slade suddenly interrupted her reverie, slanting her a lazily quizzical glance. 'Are you regretting having decided to come?'

'No, of course not!' she denied so fervently, so swiftly, that she wondered a trifle discomfitedly if she hadn't inadvertently permitted her feelings to show a little too much. 'I—I was just thinking about the dogs, that's all.'

'Including the two that were despatched overseas last week, no doubt,' he surmised drily. 'I get the feeling that if it was left to you none of them would ever be sold.'

Taryn's lips curved involuntarily at the accuracy of his assumption. 'Well, how would you like to go straight from an Australian summer to a North

American winter?' she countered with an eloquent half smile.

'Not greatly, I admit,' he grinned. 'But I expect I'd survive all the same . . . as will they. The fact that they are such a hardy animal is one of their chief selling points, after all.'

'Oh, I suppose so,' she sighed. 'It's just that . . .' She halted, eyeing him curiously. 'Don't you ever wonder if they're being well treated or not?'

'Not usually.' He shook his head negligently. 'When someone goes to the trouble and expense of purchasing a good dog—especially one that can, and will, save them a lot of work—then it's extremely unlikely they're not going to bother about caring for it properly.' His grey eyes filled with bantering amusement as they flicked over her briefly. 'So you see, there really isn't any need for you to view their sales with quite such reluctance.'

Taryn pulled an expressive face. He was probably right, of course, she conceded grudgingly, but didn't let that stop her from defending in challenging tones, 'That still won't stop me from missing them, though. Particularly little Katie.' She cast him a sidelong, openly cajoling glance. 'Are you absolutely positive you have to sell her?'

Slade's return gaze was appreciative, but unswayed. 'Uh-huh.' His confirmation was laconically drawled. 'When it comes right down to it, that's the reason she was bred, honey.'

'Heel!' she denounced, but without any sting. 'Do you always have to resort to such logical arguments?'

He laughed, an utterly captivating sound she found irresistible. 'Sorry, but emotional decisions hardly make for a sound, or successful, basis upon which to conduct a business.' A pause. 'And if it wasn't for the

dogs being a business, I wouln't have had a reason to
agree to your being employed at Merringannee in the
first place,' he reminded meaningfully.

The remark brought to mind her brother's visit
and Taryn debated whether to advise him of it, but
eventually decided against doing so. After all, despite
it having happened a week or so ago now, she still
couldn't imagine Slade being particularly pleased at
discovering Luke, of all people, had crept on to the
property secretly, or that she hadn't seen fit to
mention the occurrence at the time. An omission she
had often pondered over herself, wondering whether it
had been the right course for her to adopt. Now it
seemed too late to rectify it and she returned her
attention to the present instead.

'I guess not,' she really had no recourse but to agree
with his last observation, albeit rather wryly, and let
the matter drop.

They arrived at Tantallon, a typical country town
with wide, tree-lined streets and the usual array of
stores catering to a mainly farming community,
shortly after seven o'clock. However, as the Field Day
was to be held on one of the local properties—the only
venue both large enough to provide space for all the
equipment that would undoubtedly be on display, as
well as able to provide the tracts of land necessary for
any demonstrations by such tractors, earth-moving
machines, etcetera—it took a while longer before they
had located the actual property, and their allocated
space thereon. Although they did still manage to have
the portable yard Slade had brought with them erected
and the kennel's advertising signs displayed before the
public began arriving not long after eight.

For Taryn, the Field Day was an entirely new
experience, and she looked over the various presenta-

tions with a great deal of interest, not to mention surprise. She hadn't realised previously just how much equipment *was* available to the modern farmer and grazier. It was a whole new world as far as she was concerned and this added to her enjoyment as the crowds grew, the sun beat down hotly from an azure sky, and the day progressed.

All morning there was a knowledgeable, ever-changing group of spectators clustered around the yard where the dogs went through their paces with a handful of sheep loaned for the purpose by the property's owner, and for a time Taryn was kept busy filling in the appropriate details and getting Slade to sign the registration papers as one after another the kelpies were sold—including Katie.

'Sorry, honey,' Slade surprised her by apologising softly as he put his name to the relevant registration before handing over the pup. 'But you can rest assured she couldn't have a better owner. I've known Pierce for a good many years, as well as having sold dogs to him before, and he'll do the right thing by her the same as he does by the rest of his animals.' Then, smiling at the tall, middle-aged, and Taryn was relieved to see, kindly faced grazier next to him as he passed the document across, 'Katie's been one of Taryn's favourites,' bringing her closer to him with a hand resting casually, familiarly, against the nape of her neck, 'so you'd better take extra good care of her, Pierce, or she'll probably never forgive you.'

'I see,' Pierce chuckled good humouredly, his astute blue eyes not missing Slade's proprietorial stance. 'Well, you've no call to worry on that point, love, because I think a lot of my dogs and treat them accordingly.' His glance shifted to focus squarely on the younger man, his lips twitching expressively. 'Especially when they cost as much as this one did.'

'She's worth every penny of it and you know it, otherwise you wouldn't have bought her,' Slade defended easily with a grin.

Pierce looked down consideringly at the pup held under his arm, noting her evident desire to return to the yard to resume working the sheep, and gave a crooked smile. 'You've got me there,' he granted. 'But then you always damned well have. You breed too good a dog.' In pseudo-despair.

Having consoled herself with the thought that if Katie had to be sold then she had probably gone to the next best of masters, Taryn gazed up at Slade quizzically once the grazier had departed. 'You did up her price from what you'd originally planned, though, didn't you?'

'Mmm, just a little,' he shrugged, then fixed her with an indolent smile that devastated her every emotion. 'I figured that if she went for that amount it would only be to someone who really appreciated her, and if she didn't . . . well, it would have made at least one of us happy, wouldn't it?'

'You mean, you did it just for me?' she gasped, finding the idea both incredible and elating.

He flexed a wide shoulder again in a deprecating gesture. 'It wasn't imperative that she be sold today,' he drawled, chaffingly non-committal.

'It wasn't for the others either but you didn't raise their prices,' she pointed out slyly.

With a laughing look of surrender he finally admitted, 'Okay, so I did it for you . . . satisfied?'

'Maybe,' it was her turn to parry pertly now. But as waves of precarious excitement surged through her on seeing a roguish expression of promised retaliation sweeping across his face, circumspectly added, 'But then again, on second thoughts—yes, of course ... thank you.'

'I should think so,' he growled in mock rough tones, but there was nothing at all harsh in his touch as he trailed his fingers down the side of her throat evocatively before circumstances forced him to turn to deal with another prospective customer, and Taryn retired to the trailer because she knew that if she remained there was no way he could avoid seeing her feelings for him mirrored in her eyes.

By mid-afternoon the remainder of the dogs had also been sold, but instead of immediately packing up and leaving Slade showed Taryn round the rest of the exhibits, introducing her to the various friends and acquaintances he stopped to talk to—it seemed people came from far and near to attend field days—and generally including her in his conversations. For Taryn, it made her feel as if she had been accepted into the grazing community, of belonging almost, and she would willingly have remained doing the same all night.

For a while that did actually appear a possibility, because after having accepted an invitation from a young, married couple who were obviously long-time friends of Slade's to join them for dinner on their nearby property, they were then pressed to stay overnight as well by their hosts when their convivial conversation kept them all engaged long into the evening. However despite seeming in no more of a hurry than Taryn to have the day finally end, Slade declined the offer due to the amount of work he had planned for the morrow and they eventually took their leave just after eleven.

Tired, but totally satisfied, Taryn wasn't surprised

to find herself feeling like dozing in between her desultory exchanges with Slade on their way home, although that still didn't stop her from railing at herself after one such brief lapse, or so she had supposed, on being awakened with the advice that they had arrived at Merringannee. She hadn't wanted to miss a single minute of their time together.

'I'm sorry,' she promptly apologised self-consciously and sat up quickly on discovering her head to be resting familiarly against Slade's shoulder. 'I didn't intend to go off to sleep like that. It—it must have just crept up on me.'

'No sweat,' he shrugged idly, the hint of a quirk to his mouth quite marked as a result of one of the still-lit verandah lights spilling its golden beam into the otherwise darkened interior of the station wagon. 'Isn't that a male's role in life—to protect and provide . . . even to the extent of a shoulder for a pillow?'

Uncertain whether he was teasing her or not, she flushed. 'Yes—well—I should still have stayed awake, if only to—to help make it easier for you to do the same,' she stammered. 'I mean, no doubt you're as tired as I am, and with no one to talk to on a long journey late at night, that's when drivers can fall asleep too.'

'Though not when they're made so very aware of a shapely female form nestled extremely temptingly against them, of course.'

'Oh!' Taryn's cheeks burnt hotly now. But in a desperate effort to camouflage her embarrassment, she quipped with studied flippancy, 'Well—awake or asleep—I'm glad my presence did at least prevent us from ending up in some ditch, or worse.'

'Not that we would have, anyway,' he declaimed on

a dry, completely self-assured note, 'but I wouldn't say that's exactly how I viewed the situation.'

This time Taryn didn't answer at all—judging it wisest in view of the fact that she was only too conscious just how deeply her own feelings were involved where this man was concerned, whereas she couldn't be sure just how his were affected in return, or even if indeed they were affected at all except superficially, she had to add, no matter how desolating the thought—but began preparing to alight from the vehicle instead.

'I'll—umm—see you in the morning, then, shall I?' she turned to enquire once she was outside and ready to re-close the door, her previous thoughts making her voice sound somewhat stilted.

Momentarily, Slade simply contemplated her with a curious glance. Then, with an imperceptible hunching of a broad shoulder and mocking twist of his lips, he drawled, 'I guess so . . . unless you're not planning on rising before noon.'

'No of course I'm not,' she denied, shaking her head quickly. 'I just meant—it's just that—I mean, I didn't want to . . .' Aware she wasn't making much sense she came to an uncomfortable stop, chewing at her lip. Oh, Lord, how could she explain her sudden feeling of vulnerability in his presence when she had so enjoyed being with him during the day? She wasn't any too certain as to its origins herself, except to say that she was apprehensive of him realising how much he had come to mean to her in case she had misread his attitude after all. Nevertheless, she was evidently going to have to make some excuse, and with this in mind she forced herself to return his glance with the semblance of an unperturbed smile catching at her mouth. 'Sorry about that,' she began again with a lightly amused, though not particularly steady, laugh. 'What I was trying to say was, as it *has* been a long day, you're undoubtedly anxious to just garage the car and trailer before getting to bed, and I didn't want to delay you in any way, that's all.'

'In other words, even good days have to end sometime, hmm?'

'Something like that, I suppose,' she pounced eagerly on the assumption, and purposely ignored the somewhat sardonic inflection in his voice. Closing the door now she bent to continue through the window, 'Although I would like to thank you for making it such an interesting and pleasant one. I thought your friends were very nice too.'

'And they approved of you very highly also, honey,' came the reply, but on such a wry note that she couldn't disregard the inflection on this occasion.

In fact, she swallowed convulsively. Oh, heavens, they hadn't been doing a spot of matchmaking as his tone seemed to have implied, had they? It was not only embarrassing to contemplate, but wholly dismaying into the bargain. Not that she could do much if that had been the case, though, except to treat it as indifferently as possible.

'That was kind of them,' she therefore declared in strictly offhand accents. 'But now I really must be going in or else I will be delaying you, so I'll just say good night and let you be on your way to the garage.'

'Thanks' he acknowledged laconically, shifting the station wagon back into gear, and with a last half-awkward, half-thankful smile Taryn turned and hurried up the steps and into the house.

Thirty minutes later, after having showered and changed into a short cool nightdress, she knew she was going to have to get something to drink or she would never sleep. She didn't know whether it was something she'd eaten at dinner, the seafood perhaps, but something had given her a thirst that was demanding to be quenched immediately. So slipping on a knee-length, cotton brunch coat, she left her room and began making her way down the hall towards the stairs, surprised to see light streaming outwards from Slade's bedroom half way along the other side.

Temporarily, she considered returning to her own room, but knowing that wasn't going to relieve her thirst in the slightest, and surmising he was probably showering in any case, she continued on determinedly. Or, at least she did until she actually drew abreast of the doorway and Slade, minus his shirt but otherwise still dressed as he had been during the day, happened to choose that moment to move towards the door, whereupon she came to an abrupt halt. The sight of his bare and bronzed muscular chest somehow succeeded in making her feel extremely self-conscious regarding her own state of dress in spite of knowing full well she was adequately covered, and she rushed into speech in the hope of dispelling both disconcerting awarenesses.

'I was just going to get myself something to drink. I seem to have developed a shocking thirst all of a sudden,' she explained in a low voice to avoid disturbing either Mrs Douglas or Jeff whose rooms weren't that far distant. 'Would you like me to bring one back up for you too?' Eyeing him somewhat shyly.

'I wouldn't say no to a beer,' he acceded with a grin. 'I'm feeling a little on the dry side myself. Do you reckon it could have been the seafood?' Crooking a humorously quizzical brow.

'I must admit the thought did occur to me,' she half

laughed, and declaring that she wouldn't be long, resumed walking.

In the end it took Taryn longer than she anticipated, because unable to find any chilled tins of fruit juice, which had been her preference for quenching her thirst, she set about juicing some refrigerated oranges instead. Consequently, by the time she made her way to Slade's room with a can of beer in one hand and a tall glass of orange juice in the other, he was just emerging from his connecting bathroom with a towel knotted casually about his lithe waist after evidently having showered.

Wishing he had still been in the bathroom so she could have left the can and departed immediately, Taryn now entered the room hesitantly in order to hand the beer to him. His attire, such as it was, making her disturbingly conscious of him physically, the woman in her too ungovernably stimulated by his maleness for her peace of mind, and causing her to lick at her lips nervously.

'For the second time, I—I'll say good night, then, and leave you to enjoy your beer,' she murmured unsteadily, her accompanying and supposedly natural smile a weak facsimile of what she intended.

'What's your hurry?' Slade caught hold of her wrist lightly, but none the less securely, before she had taken more than a couple of steps towards the hallway. 'A drink is always nicer with company, and since you're only going to have yours alone in your room too ...' He shrugged expressively.

'But—but if someone should happen to pass—your mother, or Jeff even—there's no telling what they might think on—on seeing me in here,' she put forward the first excuse that entered her head.

'No worries.' Her consternation was dismissed with

drawling ease as he lifted a bare foot and pushed the door shut. 'Now no one can see who's in here.'

Taryn gulped in dismay, realising she couldn't have chosen a worse pretext. 'M-maybe not, but I—I still think it would be best if I returned to my own room all the same.' She contrived to imbue her voice with some firmness, unfortunately not very successfully, simply managing to sound even less sure of herself.

In comparison, Slade was unquestionably relaxed as, meanwhile, he took a mouthful of liquid from his can, commenting appreciatively, 'Mmm, I needed that,' before his shrewd grey eyes deliberately sought and held her slightly wary amethyst ones, and he finally responded to her last shaky demurral. 'Why? Because you're not accustomed to having a drink with a man at this time of night?'

'Not in his bedroom, no!' There was no sigh of indecisiveness in that flaring denial at least, she was pleased to note.

'So what's the difference between here and being downstairs? We'd still be alone,' he pointed out drily.

Nettled by what she suspected was a mocking intonation in his voice, as well as his unfailing self-assurance and, last but by no means least, his overwhelming magnetism, she angled her head higher to claim defensively, 'It's just different, that's all.'

'Because there's a bed instead of a settee?' he taunted openly this time.

Taryn flushed warmly and took a long swallow of her own drink now, but traitorously it only seemed to leave her mouth feeling drier. 'It has some bearing on it, naturally,' she conceded tightly at length. As also did the fact that she was finding it impossible to disregard his only partially covered form as readily as he evidently did, she admitted—but only to herself.

Suddenly his expression sobered, and the fingers that had still been clasping her wrist now trailed a tantalising path along the soft underside of her jaw. 'And especially when you know as well as I do that we've been heading towards a moment just such as this all day, hmm?'

'No, I . . .' She began to refute protectively, only to break off in nervous confusion when he leant past her in order to place his can on a table just behind her. Conversely, she clutched at her own glass more tightly, holding it in front of her as if it was a shield of some kind as she took a hasty step backwards.

With both his hands free now it presented no problem to Slade to cup her face between them swiftly, however. 'Who are you trying to deceive, honey? Me . . . or yourself?' he probed as he bent his head closer.

'Neither!' she disputed in something of a panic and doing her best to avoid his still lowering mouth. If he kissed her she would be lost. She knew that as surely as night followed day. For feeling about him as she did, she doubted her strength of will would be sufficient to make anything but the most token of stands against such a provoking onslaught. Drawing a ragged breath, she made an effort to continue. 'I'm merely . . .'

'Reluctant to admit that you're not as indifferent as you'd like to appear?' he inserted subtly as he resolutely relieved her of her glass and deposited it on the table next to his can.

Taryn caught at her lip with pearly white teeth in dismay, knowing she could never deny such a deduction, and despairing of the fact that most of her emotions were already responding to his disturbing proximity anyway.

'Or haven't you realised I've been wanting to do this all day?' he continued on a thickening note as he at last set his lips to hers with possessive determination.

A wayward feeling of warmth promptly swept through Taryn, her whole body quivering at his touch as he drew her closer to his darky tanned chest, and although she initially attempted to strain away from him it was really only a momentary effort. Now that she was actually in his arms she was as lost to reason as she had predicted, because in the inner recesses of her mind she knew she just didn't want to be anywhere else. And having confessed as much, if only inwardly, she pressed even more compliantly against his virile frame, her fingers gliding pleasurably over the rippling muscles of his powerful back, her mouth fervently returning the vitally stirring pressure of his.

With a smothered groan, Slade gathered her into his arms and carried her across to the bed, catching her to him again as he stretched out his vibrantly masculine length beside her. His hands moved in a slow, smooth, unending caress of her curving body, arousing within her a throbbing desire she had never before encountered, but which had her moving against him enticingly.

Only half aware of the buttons on her brunch coat being undone, Taryn made no demur when he slipped it from her slender shoulders altogether, or when he then proceeded to remove the barrier that was her nightdress in the same sensuous fashion. She wanted to experience his warm, firm skin touching hers, to savour his unimpeded touch, and to lovingly explore the contours of his rugged form in return.

It seemed that now the controls on her emotions had been released, she could withhold nothing, but even so she still trembled convulsively when his skilfully caressing hands cradled her swelling breasts and his shapely mouth sought the rapidly beating hollow of her throat before travelling leisurely downwards until her every nerve exploded with an aching longing as it finally captured a taut and full nipple. Gasping at the depths of passion he had stimulated, her violet-blue eyes, dark and filled with emotion, slowly opened to gaze up at him with smouldering fervour.

'Oh, God, I love you!' she breathed throatily, the words slipping out of their own volition.

With a harsh, abrupt movement that took her completely by surprise, Slade suddenly rolled away from her to lay staring up at the ceiling with his hands linked behind his tousled head. 'Then I suggest you get out of here before I change my mind and make love to you as I originally planned!' he bit out on a hard note without looking at her.

Oblivious to her nakedness, Taryn eased herself into a sitting position, her frowning countenance reflecting her total bewilderment. 'But I wanted you to make love to me,' she owned with a simple, if a trifle self-conscious, honesty.

'Well, I've decided I don't!' His rejection slashed at her stingingly.

But he *had* wanted to, she knew he had! She wasn't so inexperienced that she couldn't tell he'd been as aroused as she was. Lifting a hand to her temple she began rubbing at it as if it ached. 'B-because I said I loved you?' she quavered in a dismal whisper. That was when he'd called a halt, after all.

He gave the smallest of shrugs. 'I guess you could say that.'

'Wh-why?' she just had to ask, then bit at her lip to

still its sudden trembling.

A muscle jerked at the side of his tautly held jaw as he slanted her a darkly savage gaze that had her clutching her nightdress to her chest as if for protection. 'Because I figured that made my revenge just about complete,' he divulged in mockingly acid tones.

Taryn went cold, feeling as if a knife had just been plunged into her. 'R-revenge?' she repeated with an uncontrollable shiver.

'Mmm, in return for the treatment meted out by you and your brother,' he smiled mirthlessly. 'It might make you think twice about trying the same trick on some other family in future.'

'But I've already told you I wasn't . . .' She came to a despairing stop, her shoulders drooping, her eyes becoming veiled with tears of hurt. If he hadn't believed her before, she was only wasting her time attempting to convince him of her innocence now. 'Luke said I was a fool for wanting anything to do with you,' she recalled half disconsolately, half bitterly. 'Apparently he was right.'

'Oh? And when did he say that?' Slade probed on a coldly suspicious note, propping himself up on his elbows the better to watch her.

'When he came to see me a week ago,' she revealed reluctantly, remembering she hadn't mentioned the visit before.

'A secret rendezvous obviously!' he grated in a mixture of anger and contempt. 'Which merely confirms everything I've said! So what plan did the pair of you devise this time? Was this all a part of it too?' Indicating the rumpled bed with a jeering nod of his head. 'In the hope that I would succumb to your—er—undoubted charms to the extent where I'd be defenceless against your schemes to relieve this family of even more money?'

'No!' she sobbed in protest, her tears beginning to stream down her abnormally pale cheeks now. 'It wasn't anything like that! He simply came to offer me the money I needed to repay you!'

'Duped another sucker out of some, had he?'

She shook her head miserably in negation. 'No, he won it on the horses.'

'Yeah, I can imagine,' he gibed, totally unbelieving. 'So where is this money, then?'

'I didn't accept it,' dully.

'Thought you were on a better thing remaining here, did you?'

A defensive numbness started to overtake Taryn, but before it enveloped her completely her still brimming eyes flashed with momentary acrimony as she recollected just why she had chosen not to leave. 'You wouldn't believe me even if I did say otherwise,' she charged.

'With good reason, evidently!'

There didn't seem much point in replying so she merely located her brunch coat and, partly turning away from him, shrugged into it. With her fingers still clenching at her nightdress she then pulled the coat tightly around herself and, keeping her arms wrapped about her midriff as if for support, rose slowly to her feet.

'Then, if that's all you . . .' she murmured listlessly, wanting only the protective solitude of her own room now.

'Not quite,' Slade disallowed curtly. 'You can also forget about the dogs in the morning.'

Her thickly framed lavender eyes lifted to his slowly. 'You're firing me?' she surmised expressionlessly. After all that had happened, nothing he said would have surprised her.

'Hardly!' he half laughed on a caustic note. 'You still owe me a considerable amount of money. Or were you hoping I'd cancel the balance in view of your having proved yourself such a responsive bed partner?' A taunting eyebrow rose.

Deep colour washed into Taryn's cheeks, the vivid stain made all the more noticeable due to the unnatural pallor of the rest of her face, but once again she refrained from answering, countering instead, 'Th-then what . . .?'

'Will you be doing?' he supplied for her. 'Since Mother's apparently having difficulty keeping her committee paperwork up to date again, you can help her for the remainder of your time here. Think you can manage it?' Up went both brows in mocking unison this time.

So he was intent on making her life as difficult as possible, was he? The thought had a spark of challenge abruptly flashing in her eyes and her chin lifting marginally higher. 'I don't see why not. At least your Mother's honest enough to show her dislike. She doesn't p-pretend to be f-friendly,' her voice began to crack under the strain and she had to exert every ounce of willpower to prevent it continuing in the same vein, 'solely for the purpose of inflicting greater pain when it's least anticipated!' she slated as she whirled for the door and flung it open. 'To do that you have to be a real bastard, Slade, and in that regard neither your Mother nor anyone else could ever hope to compete with you!' And with a choking cry of anguish she fled down the hall to the refuge of her room.

Once there, however, and now that the deadness of

feeling that had been sustaining her had started to wear off, unbidden tears made their welling reappearance as she threw herself down on to her bed and wept brokenly. She felt cheap and humiliated, hurt and desolated, her emotions lacerated and raw. It also seemed her instincts had been totally wrong from the beginning, too. It hadn't been his Mother and Ilona he'd wanted to avenge himself on by employing her— it had been her naïve, blindly unsuspecting self!

Oh, God, she didn't know how she could possibly face him again! The mortification, the wretchedness of knowing he knew she would willingly have given herself to him, and been summarily rejected, when all the time his only intention had been to lull her into just such a situation so he could exact his retaliation in the most devastating fashion possible, was more than she could stand.

Luke! All at once her brother's name catapulted into Taryn's mind, and the promise he'd made to her. Yes, that was what she would do! She would write to him first thing in the morning requesting him to pay off the balance owing to Slade as he'd offered. It was the perfect solution, and by determinedly forcing herself to concentrate on the relief she would experience on leaving Merringannee, she was eventually able to drift into, if not dreamless, then at least partially healing, sleep.

CHAPTER EIGHT

FOR the next three days Taryn felt as if she was living in a world of make-believe as she tried to appear utterly indifferent to Slade's presence—on those occasions when she couldn't avoid him entirely, that was—to also act as if she was quite amenable to working inside with Mrs Douglas—which, thankfully, at least hadn't actually proved as difficult as she had expected—while all the time in private doing her utmost to ignore the anguish that still gripped her as a result of both Slade's decimating form of reprisal and the knowledge that, in spite of everything, he still had the power to make her heart race erratically whenever she saw him.

All her hopes were now pinned on a reply from Luke to the letter she had indeed written to him and placed in with those of Mrs Douglas for posting in Jinda Jinda the very next afternoon, and although she was aware it was too soon for him to have even received it yet, let alone send an answer, she was already finding herself awaiting each day's mail collection with feverish anxiety. So much so, apparently, that it became obvious, for when Jeff returned from town with it late the following morning and left it with his mother for her and Taryn to open, Mrs Douglas remarked upon it.

'You're expecting something important, aren't you?' she hazarded after watching Taryn sort through the pile swiftly with keenly scanning eyes.

Since to date she hadn't usually shown such

eagerness when letters from her mother had arrived, there seemed little for Taryn to do but nod and own, 'Yes, as a matter of fact I am.'

'From your family?'

Surprised at the sudden interest shown by the older woman, Taryn answered unthinkingly. 'Yes, my brother.' Then, remembering Mrs Douglas didn't exactly harbour any generous feelings towards Luke, angled her head higher, as if defying any censuring of him.

On noting the gesture, Bernadette Douglas's lips twisted obliquely. 'You're very loyal to your family, aren't you, Taryn?' she merely mused speculatively, however.

If she had been surprised before, Taryn was more like astonished now. Not only because a comment regarding her brother *hadn't* been forthcoming, but also because it was the first time the other woman had ever called her anything but Miss Rodgers. In consequence, it had her stammering somewhat lamely, 'I—I guess so.'

Bernadette Douglas leant back in her chair on the opposite side of the desk they were sharing in her study, her silvery eyes viewing the finely formed, but slightly pale features across from her intently. 'And my son? Does it extend to him also?'

Taryn looked away quickly, her expression unconsciously saddening. It had once, but now . . . Now she was only increasingly apprehensive of the reason behind the question. Turning back again, she executed a briefly depreciating shrug. 'I doubt he's interested whether it does or not, Mrs Douglas,' she therefore saw fit to evade, but at least without insulting the other woman's intelligence by pretending not to know just which of her sons she had been referring to. A moment's hesitation, and she added warily, 'Why do you ask?'

'Because I'm not so involved with my own interests that I'm completely unaware of what's happening around me,' was the rather tersely voiced reply that had Taryn's stomach constricting.

'Meaning?' On a stiff, barely audible note.

A long—annoyed?—exhalation, and, 'That for the last few days there has been a barely suppressed feeling of simmering tension between you and Slade and I want to know why!'

'I'd have thought you would be only too pleased about it to care,' Taryn blurted out her innermost thoughts impulsively.

'Which merely proves how little you know me!' There was a hint of tartness in the retort. 'In any event, you're simply attempting to divert my attention.'

'Then maybe you should ask . . .'

'I already have!' came the noticeably disgruntled interruption. 'And I may as well have saved my breath! It was like trying to extract information from a brick wall! A circumstance, I might add, I've never encountered with my eldest son before.' A pause. 'So as he refuses to tell me, I'm trusting you will . . . if only in order that I might be allowed to know just what *is* causing such awkwardness in my home!'

Momentarily, Taryn rebelled against the idea. When all was said and done, in view of the trouble Mrs Douglas had tried to cause her previously, why should she be the one to assist her now? Then again, what had she got to lose? followed the dismal thought. Matters couldn't possibly deteriorate any further, and in any case she would be gone from the property very shortly once Luke lived up to his promise. Tilting her head fractionally higher she made herself hold the other woman's gaze valiantly.

'I discovered, in a somewhat demoralising fashion, that he was still of the opinion that I had somehow been involved when my brother acted so—umm—deplorably at the show,' she relayed in brittle accents.

'Demoralising fashion? You mean, he purposely—er—led you on before doing so?' shrewdly.

Fearing she had revealed too much—the last thing she wanted was for everyone to know how Slade had first fooled and then rebuffed her—Taryn shifted restively on her seat. 'What makes you think that?' she tried to bluff her way out with a weak half laugh.

'Oh, don't play me for a fool, Taryn!' she was adjured testily. 'It's patently clear something of the kind happened! Just the fact that you changed overnight from obviously welcoming my son's company to avoiding it like the plague indicates something drastic occurred, even if what you've said still isn't a particularly satisfactory explanation as to why *he's* been storming around with a face as black as thunder ever since!'

'I wouldn't know about that,' Taryn declared woodenly. As she hadn't exactly felt disposed to analyse Slade's reaction, there really wasn't much she could offer on the subject—even if she cared to. 'But if—if you don't mind, Mrs Douglas, I'd really rather not . . .'

'Discuss the matter any further?' came the interposing surmise. 'No, I'm sure you wouldn't, but unfortunately I do mean to get to the bottom of this before it goes any further, I can assure you! And, as I'm sure you will agree, I can be extremely determined when I choose.'

Wasn't that the truth! despaired Taryn, and waited

apprehensively with her head bowed for the inevitable since it was more than apparent Bernadette Douglas didn't mean to allow anything to thwart her purpose.

'So . . .' she continued in a slightly less daunting tone. 'Perhaps we can shorten this if you'll just answer me one question truthfully. Will you do that?'

Taryn touched her teeth to her lip uneasily, but didn't look up. She wanted to qualify that it would depend on what she was asked, but very much doubted that would be acceptable. 'I-I'll try,' she compromised shakily in lieu.

'Then what I would like to know is . . . are you in love with my son?'

Now Taryn did look up, rapidly. The unexpectedness, the baldness, the very unruffled manner in which the question had been voiced making her lavender eyes widen in astonishment. But as for replying, that was something else again. It was impossible to tell from Bernadette Douglas's expression just how she viewed the possibility, and as a result Taryn dropped her gaze to her tightly entwined fingers in her lap again before answering. 'I was . . . but now I don't honestly know any more,' she shocked herself by owning in a disconsolate whisper.

'And Slade?' quietly. 'How does he . . .'

'No!' The denial was hurled out vehemently. 'Oh, no, he doesn't love *me*, if that's what you were going to ask! So, you see, you've nothing to fear about him becoming involved with someone from my unexceptional station in life! No, I'm all right for making a fool of and taking revenge on, but that's as far as it goes!' She halted abruptly, gasping in dismay at what she had unintentionally divulged, but at the same time refusing to allow the tears that were stinging her eyes to fall and thereby add to her humiliation. Instead she raised her chin defiantly. 'And the reason he's out of sorts at the moment is probably because he took exception to me calling him a bastard . . . even though that's precisely what he is!'

Bernadette Douglas released a heavy breath. 'So it would appear, I'm afraid,' she granted regretfully—to her listener's almost open-mouthed amazement. 'Which is rather strange really, because in view of his behaviour the night of Shirley's party, and more especially his attitude towards you since then, I was under the impression he was beginning to care for you and that I, in turn, may have been a little too hasty in my own judgment where you were concerned. So, you see,' she copied Taryn's own words in wry tones, 'it wasn't because I objected to his becoming involved with you that I was interested to know exactly how he felt about you, but rather the opposite in fact. It was due to my being of the opinion that perhaps you could have fitted in to this family quite well.' After a slight pause—during which Taryn was far too occupied in trying to recover from the shock of what she'd just heard to even think of speaking, anyway—she went on, 'Which leads me to another point . . .' Here she halted again, her normally assured composure appearing to desert her somewhat as she first cleared her throat and then kept clasping and unclasping her hands. 'I would like you to accept my apology for having falsely accused you of stealing my earrings solely in an effort to have you dismissed,' in an obviously discomfited rush. It was plain apologising didn't come easily to her. 'It was a most shameful display of self-interest on my part, and I can assure you I've regretted having allowed myself to be persuaded to sink to such depths ever since. My only excuse, poor as it may be, is that at the time I truly believed Ilona would make Slade the most suitable wife, and being so set in my determination to prove it I foolishly also permitted her to convince me that your presence was the only thing standing in the way of their marriage and that, therefore, any means justified the end if it resulted in your departure.' Her expression assumed a remorsefully self-mocking cast. 'If I hadn't been so obstinately resolved to see my own plans come to fruition, I probably would have realised then on hearing her reasoning that she wasn't the type I should have been wanting my son to marry. However, that still doesn't excuse me for having acted upon the suggestion and for that I hope you'll believe me when I say I'm deeply sorry.'

Only just having managed to overcome her previous incredulity, Taryn now found herself faced with an even more staggering revelation to assimilate, and for a moment she could only favour the woman on the other side of the desk with a slightly bemused stare.

'Yes, well, I guess all of us allow our better judgment to be overridden at some time or another,' she conceded eventually, an ironic curve shaping her lips. 'Mine certainly was when I let myself be deluded into believing Slade no longer considered me in the same light as he did my brother. It just didn't occur to me he was simply playing a part for his own nefarious purposes.' Her mouth drooped wistfully.

'A circumstance which, without wishing to appear to doubt you at all, as I said, I must admit I still do find difficult to credit,' Bernadette Douglas revealed with a frown. 'It's just so uncharacteristic for Slade to act in such a manner.'

Taryn made a despondently resigned face. 'Maybe I merely have the unfortunate knack of rubbing the Douglas family the wrong way.'

'Except that in Slade's case . . .'

'He was cunningly going about achieving his own ends, unknown to any of us,' Taryn broke in to maintain, refusing to believe or even listen to any contentions suggesting otherwise. 'And now,' with a rather pleading half smile as she rubbed her fingertips across her forehead, 'I really would prefer to drop the subject, Mrs Douglas. I think it's just about been exhausted, in any event, and there is all this mail still waiting to be attended to.'

'Mmm, I suppose you're right, although . . .' picking up a couple of letters, glancing at them, and then dropping them again, 'I must say I don't particularly feel like doing much with them at the moment, so how about we give them a miss for today? I suspect it might do more good if you got away from the property for a while too. You've only left it twice since you've been here and you never know that a trip to Jinda Jinda, or perhaps one of the National Parks nearby, may just help you feel a little better. The drive might put some colour back in your cheeks at least, if nothing else. Take the station wagon, the keys should be in it, and I doubt anyone will be requiring it again today.'

It sounded very temping though Taryn still felt obliged to question, 'You're sure?' But on receiving a decisive confirmation, 'Then, thank you, it's very kind of you to suggest it.' Gaining her feet, she hesitated momentarily before actually taking her leave. 'I would also like to thank you for your apology and your understanding. I didn't really expect . . .'

'To receive either from an autocratic tartar like me?' Bernadette Douglas cut in to surmise whimsically. 'No, don't try and protest,' came the dry direction on seeing she was about to be interrupted, 'because although that may not have been quite what you were going to say, under the circumstances I'd be surprised if you had considered me anything else. I'm afraid I *do* have a tendency to be too domineering and arrogant, as my sons are fond of telling me, but that was the manner in which I was raised and unfortunately I'm a little too set in my ways to change now. All I *can* offer in my own defence is, as most people thankfully perceive once they get to know me, my bark is usually worse than my bite.'

Just as Jeff had once said, Taryn recalled. Aloud, and feeling more at ease in the older woman's presence than she had ever done before, she smiled, 'So I'm beginning to realise.'

Nevertheless, after having returned to her room a few minutes later in order to change out of the belted frock she had been wearing into a sleeveless blue shirt and a pair of canvas jeans, Taryn's relaxed feeling very soon disappeared as she mused over her conversation with Slade's mother while making her way slowly down the stairs. Now a form of almost mirthful hysteria assailed her as the full impact of the situation sank in. It appeared she had somehow succeeded in winning over the mother, but not the son! Oh, God, what a hideous irony! It wasn't that she hadn't wanted to establish a more congenial relationship with Mrs Douglas, but it was Slade who had come to mean so much to her, *just Slade!* she despaired brokenly.

As if her thoughts of him had prompted it, Taryn suddenly heard Slade's voice unexpectedly issuing from the office towards the back of the house and, anxious as ever to avoid him, she immediately darted in the opposite direction. To emerge on to the front verandah just as Ilona alighted from her car parked in the driveway and began moving towards the steps.

Putting two and two together—the dark blonde-headed girl's so very confident expression, plus Slade's uncustomary presence in the homestead at that time of day—she could only deduce that Ilona was there at his invitation, but despite the stab of pain in her chest that the notion engendered, she prepared to greet the other girl with as much unconcern as she could valiantly muster.

As it was, it was Ilona who spoke first. Although not by any stretch of the imagination could her remark have been classified as a greeting. 'You should have listened to me,' she began with a smirk. 'I told you his stooping to bed you wouldn't mean he'd wed you, didn't I?'

Taryn could hardly believe her ears, and nor could she prevent her face from flaming hotly. That Slade should evidently have informed the other girl what had occurred was just too mortifying to be borne, not to mention being callously despicable! Just how much more revenge did he intend to exact before he would be satisfied?

'Except that he didn't happen to bed me either,' she at last managed to dispute on recovering a little. 'So it would appear you've been misled somewhat, wouldn't it?'

'Oh, I don't think so,' refuted Ilona smugly as they both reached the top of the steps. 'Particularly in view of that give-away colour staining your face so brilliantly. Besides, it was a foregone conclusion, anyway, that he would dump you the minute he'd got what he wanted from you. I mean, not even you could have been so stupidly optimistic as to think he would consider anything else except a short affair with someone as unsuitable as you!' With a maliciously denigrating tinkle of laughter. 'Or were you?'

'No, as a matter of fact I wasn't,' Taryn was pleased to be able to deny, but even more pleased to add mockingly, 'Although Mrs Douglas was, apparently.' There, that should take the supercilious look off her face!

Did it ever! 'Bernadette did?' Ilona expostulated incredulously. 'I don't believe you! She would never countenance anyone like you in her family! You're just saying that in an attempt to cause more trouble between us!' Her brown eyes glittered venomously.

'Why should I bother? You seem more than capable of doing that all by yourself,' Taryn wasn't above taunting.

'Is that so?' Ilona spat. 'Well, there's something else I'm more than capable of doing by myself too, I'll have you know, and that will be to personally have you tossed off this property the minute I'm mistress here! So how smart do you feel now, you scheming little bitch?'

Taryn shrugged, expressively indifferent, then followed it with an equally meaningful, '*If* you become mistress here, of course!' From what Bernadette Douglas had had to say on the subject, she somehow doubted Ilona had an ally there any more to help her achieve her desire.

'Oh, there's no question about that, it's only a matter of time,' Ilona patently felt confident enough to boast in a return to her most disdainful manner. 'After all, it *was* Slade's idea that I came over today, and even you would have to admit that we are an extremely well-matched, as well as striking, pair.'

'Mmm, in the mould of Caesare and Lucretia Borgia,' quipped Taryn with an eloquent grimace. 'By all accounts, they were an extremely well-matched and *striking*,' with sardonic emphasis, 'pair too!' She tilted her head in feigned consideration. 'Yes, I'd say the pair of you would have no trouble whatsoever being just as ruthless and coldblooded as they ever were.'

Ilona's lips thinned, and she thrust her face forward threateningly. 'Then you'd better take care I don't start with you, hadn't you?'

'Since I don't anticipate being here much longer . . .'

'You mean, Slade's already fired you?' Ilona surmised in a gloating tone.

'No, it's all my own decision,' Taryn disabused her with an airiness she was really far from feeling as she now started to descend the steps. 'I simply found I couldn't stomach some of the people I met round here any more.' Passing her eyes up and down the other girl's form significantly.

'Why, you . . .!' The furious ejaculation came from behind Taryn as Ilona turned to follow her, and then a hand forcefully thumping into her back sent her sprawling down the remaining steps and on to the ground below. 'That's the only place for the likes of you! In the dirt!' Ilona crowed.

On her feet again in a flash, Taryn's own emotions suddenly soared, and without even giving herself time to think she reacted as she never had in her life before. She let fly with a clenched fist straight for Ilona's exulting face and which, on connecting with the blonde's eye, sat her back on the steps with a howl of rage rather than pain.

'Slade! *Slade*!' Ilona immediately screamed at the top of her voice. 'Help me! This uncontrolled slut you call an employee has just attacked me! Slade, please! *Help me*!' Her voice grew even more shrill.

Hearing footsteps fast approaching the doorway, accompanied by an explosively rapped, 'What in hell . . .!'

Taryn decided it would be prudent to make herself scarce and disappeared round the corner of the homestead swiftly. It was doubtful Ilona even noticed her leaving so concerned was she with creating just the right effect as she draped herself dramatically across the steps holding one hand to her eye, the other to her chest, and uttering suitable moans of distress.

'*Taryn!*'

Hearing herself summoned in a strident bark a few seconds later, Taryn gave a defiant toss of her head, refusing to heed it, and continued on her way to the garage. Even if she hadn't acted in a very prudent fashion, she wasn't going to have Slade bawling her out in front of Ilona Welbourne . . . no way! And nor would she be apologising either! Ilona had had it in for her from the moment they met and, as far as Taryn was concerned, she had merely paid her back a little on account. In any event, the other girl had been the first to resort to physical measures, so she had no one to blame but herself if she had received more than she bargained for in return! She rationalised defensively.

On reaching the garage Taryn slid behind the wheel of the station wagon thoughtfully, debating just where she should go. To drive in to Jinda Jinda, or anywhere that necessitated using the main highway, for that matter, meant she would have to pass the front of the homestead and since that presented the possibility of being stopped by Slade the idea didn't exactly appeal greatly. Rather than have that happen she would travel in the opposite direction, she decided, reversing out of the garage now, and by cutting through the back paddocks explore some of the still uncleared areas of mallee instead.

It was a part of the property she had only seen once when Slade had taken her with him to check out a water pump, but the timeless, almost untouched aura it had generated had somehow filled her with a feeling of satisfying serenity and she hoped today's visit might accomplish the same. Lord knew, she felt in need of something to soothe her torn and aching thoughts and emotions, she sighed dispiritedly as she kept the vehicle following the sandy track that led westwards. She might even make it to the bluff that had given the property its name, and which Slade had pointed out to her in the distance that day, because if she took care she couldn't see why she shouldn't be able to make it that far. Of course, Merringannee Bluff had an entirely different connotation for her these days, her musings rolled on with inexorable desolation, for Slade's ploy had certainly been the most destructive bluff she could ever have envisaged.

Presently, after having passed through another three mammoth paddocks and each time having to stop to open and then re-close their gates behind her, Taryn found the landscape beginning to alter markedly. Gone now were the wide open spaces as the scrub progressively became thicker, the red sand forming the track deeper and less well-packed. This was close to the edge of desert country, and although there were some taller trees visible periodically, most of the growth was yellow, white, and narrow-leaved red mallee—slender, but many-stemmed variations of eucalyptus of compact, bushy habit that formed thickets, some almost impenetrable, rather than stands and whose wood was too hard to cut even with an axe.

It was extremely hot, dry, and Taryn discovered on venturing further into it, somewhat forbidding country despite the peacefulness it exuded and which had so attracted her previously. Because by virtue of its very flatness and closely surrounding bush, it tended to make it almost impossible to discern any landmarks whatsoever, and if she hadn't just happened to be looking in the right direction when a brief gap allowed a glimpse of the broad bluff she was seeking, she doubted she would have gone much further before turning back.

As it was, she was just about having to choose her own route now, the track she had been following seeming to have petered out some miles back, but now that she had a better idea in which direction to head, she pressed on with renewed confidence. Her only regret was that she hadn't thought to bring anything to eat, or perhaps more appropriately, to drink with her because she was definitely starting to feel both would have been most welcome.

However, on finding the scrub abruptly clearing a short while later, Taryn just as suddenly forgot all about eating and drinking in seeing the bluff clearly ahead of her, while to her left the flat ground gave way to a succession of rolling, red sand-hills whipped into shape by successive southeasterly winds, their sides and ridges adorned with yellow grasses, stunted bushes, and trailing creepers.

It was a magnificent scene, the vividness of the colours as the overpowering red of the sand met the intense blue of the sky an incredible sight, but in her eagerness to reach the bluff and from its summit perhaps view the panorama better, she forgot to pay as much attention to cautiously selecting her route as she had been doing before, with the result that in attempting to breast one particular ridge the station wagon suddenly sank up to its axles in the loose sand and no amount of effort on her part could succeed in freeing it.

Disgusted with herself for having been so stupidly

careless, Taryn stood looking at the stranded vehicle
indecisively for a moment. Now what was she
supposed to do? Walk all the way back to the
homestead, or wait where she was in the hope someone
else would come along? She was well aware that in
most cases it was recommended one always remained
with the car, their bulk being more easily spotted from
above if an aerial search was instituted, for one thing,
but since no one knew she had come out here, anyway,
plus the fact that she hadn't noticed any signs of
recent tyre marks for the last ten miles or more, she
considered she really had little choice but to reject the
latter option.

Shrugging philosophically, she supposed it was
going to have to be the decidedly unappealing long
walk, after all, but which she trusted maybe wouldn't
be too bad if she waited until the hottest part of the
day was over before commencing her trek. While in
the meantime ... Gazing at the bluff speculatively,
she gave a nod as if having made up her mind. It
seemed a pity if, after having managed to get this close
to it, she didn't at least make an effort to climb it, she
decided, and promptly set off towards the rather
steep-sided hill, intending to do just that.

In the end, though, just the walk across to its base
under the blazing sun had her shirt starting to cling to
her in places with perspiration and, exchanging
adventure for discretion, she deemed her desire for
climbing to have wilted along with herself and instead
found a thankfully shaded niche behind a rock where
she could more comfortably rest until it was time to
leave.

CHAPTER NINE

TARYN guessed she must have dozed off because the next thing she knew someone was calling out to her and, combing her fingers absently through her copper-coloured hair as she pushed herself away from the rock a little, she noticed that the area of shade she had been sheltering in had lengthened considerably. Then the call came again, and recognising Slade's resonant voice she pulled a disgruntled face but still neither replied nor moved into view. Why he should have been out there she had no idea, particularly when he had Ilona all too willing to keep him company at the homestead. Unless, of course . . . she was with him! the dismaying thought promptly ensued. The unpalatable notion had her inching forward to peer around the rock in order to check—and found herself staring squarely at Slade's towering, denim-clad figure as he reached her concealed position.

'Why in blazes didn't you answer?' he immediately clipped out in rough tones. 'I've been searching for you for hours! Are you all right?'

'Yes, thank you,' she replied stiffly to his last query first, her eyes flicking past him to where he had brought his ute to rest not far from the station wagon, and then swinging back again with relief at knowing Ilona apparently hadn't been invited along. 'H-how did you know I was here?' She looked up with a frown creasing her forehead.

'Tracks,' he relayed shortly, indicating the notice-able footprints in the sand leading from the vehicles.

'The same way I eventually located the car once Burt had returned to the homestead and said he'd seen you heading in this direction earlier. Up until then, after checking that no one had seen you either on the way to Jinda Jinda, or anywhere thereabouts, I hadn't a clue where you might have been.' He paused, his grey eyes unfathomable as he gazed down at her unwaveringly. 'So why didn't you answer when you heard me calling?'

Taryn hunched an excusing shoulder. 'I think I must have been half asleep the first time.'

'You obviously weren't the second, though, were you?'

'I—well . . .' She averted her gaze but remained seated, linking her arms about her upraised knees. 'Just because you're evidently so anxious, and willing to go to such lengths to read me a lecture, I saw no reason why I should make it easier for you to do so,' she defended mutinously.

Slade rested his hands on lean hips. 'And what makes you so sure that was my intention?'

'You know damned well why!' The hot words burst forth in spontaneous resentment for his cat-and-mouse tactics. 'Because I had the unforgivable temerity not to accept either your girlfriend's verbal or physical abuse without retaliating, of course! Why else would you have bothered to look for me all afternoon otherwise?'

'Maybe because I was as worried as hell about you when you'd been gone for so long and nobody seemed to know where you were, and . . .'

'*You* . . . worried about *me*!' she cut him off with a gibing half laugh. 'Oh, don't try giving me that, Slade! You may have been capable of making me believe it once, but never again, believe me . . . n-never a-again!' An ignominious break started to appear in her voice and she turned away, pressing her lips together resolutely. 'In any case,' she made a concentrated effort to keep it steady this time, 'no matter what the reason it won't make much difference to me very shortly, I'm glad to say.'

'Oh?' His brows peaked interestedly.

'That's right.' Her expression took on a challenging look. 'You see I've sent a letter to Luke asking him to pay off the remainder of his debt, after all, and once that happens there's no way on earth I'll be remaining on Merringannee one single minute longer than is absolutely necessary!'

Returning her openly exultant glance imperturbably, Slade sank down on to the sand beside her. 'The only flaw in that plan being ... I guessed as much when I chanced to see your letter among the others waiting to be posted so I—er—took the liberty of removing it. Sorry, honey, but it was never mailed,' he advised lazily.

'Not mailed!' Disappointment and rage mingled so fiercely within Taryn that she launched herself at him in a flurry of pummelling fists. 'Oh, you vile, detestable bastard!' she stormed bitterly. 'How dare you interfere with my letters! *How dare you!*'

For his part, Slade made short work of capturing her flailing hands within an iron grip, his shapely mouth curving surprisingly into an amused smile. 'My, you really are feeling physical today, aren't you?' he drawled.

Not unexpectedly, the thought that he found the situation humorous did nothing to mollify Taryn's feelings of outrage and her breasts rose and fell sharply as her wrath failed to abate. 'You don't know the half of it! But you will the minute you let go of me!' she threatened, eyes smouldering.

'Thanks for the warning.' He dipped his head mockingly. 'Perhaps I'd better make certain I don't release you, then, hmm?'

'You'll have to some time!'

'Although only when I see fit, of course. And that may not be for a considerable while.'

'Meaning?' She glared at him balefully.

Before she could even move to hinder, let alone stop him, he swiftly changed his grip on her hands, pinning them behind her back with only one of his own now, the other brushing across her cheek lightly before sliding into her hair and inexorably tilting her belligerent features up to his.

'Meaning, I've no intention of letting you go at all, honey,' he declared decisively and set his mouth to hers with a hungry sensuousness that had her panicking.

No, he couldn't do this to her! her mind protested frantically. She wasn't something to be used when he felt like it and then cruelly discarded until the next time! She wouldn't respond, *she wouldn't*! But no matter how she attempted to prevent it, in the end her unruly emotions defeated her, and as the hand pinioning her wrists urged her closer Taryn knew herself to be surrendering, her arms going round him compulsively, her clinging lips revealing a hunger of their own, and a sob of part desire, part despair escaped her. In spite of the way he had treated her it seemed she still loved him, wanted him, as much as ever.

'Dear God, Taryn, I can't let you go! I love you more than my life!' Slade suddenly vowed hoarsely into her tousled hair as he clasped her to him tightly. 'How could I ever have been so blind as not to have realised it sooner!'

A week ago there wasn't anything Taryn wouldn't have given to have heard him say those words, but now she steeled herself against it as she determinedly eased away from him. 'S-so what's different now? Or is this just some n-new plan of r-revenge?' she pushed out unevenly, bitterly.

Slade raked a hand through his dark hair distractedly, and expelled a deep breath. 'I guess I deserved that, didn't I?' he allowed in heavy tones. Then, more urgently as he cupped her face gently between his hands, 'But there is no more plan of revenge, honey, I swear!' Pausing, his mouth shaped ruefully, but his eyes contained a humble light she had never imagined seeing there. 'Only of loving, and caring, and marriage. That is . . . if you'll have me.'

Momentarily, Taryn's heart flooded with happiness . . . and then apprehension returned. 'To leave someone standing at the church would just about make the ultimate form of reprisal, wouldn't it? Or is Ilona perhaps presuming too much, too soon again?' Her winged brows arched sardonically.

'Uh-uh!' He shook his head unequivocally. 'This has nothing whatsoever to do with Ilona. And for your information, she was firmly shown the door again only a short time after arriving.' One corner of his mouth twitched wryly. 'Materialising black eye, and all.'

Taryn bit at her lip guiltily, but refused to be distracted. 'Then why invite her over in the first place?'

His mouth levelled expressively. 'I didn't. She rang me last night, ostensibly on behalf of her brother because, once again, he was supposedly out at the time, to find out a convenient time for him to come over today. Only, as you know, it *wasn't* Gary who arrived!'

It sounded just the thing Ilona was capable of doing, and yet ... 'She still knew about that—that night in your bedroom, though, didn't she?'

'Did she?' he countered, looking at her somewhat askance. 'I wouldn't know how.' Followed hastily by a frowning, 'My God, you don't think I'd go round revealing something like that, do you?'

She hunched a non-committal shoulder. 'It could have added to your sense of retaliation,' she proposed in a small voice. 'And who else could have told her? I certainly didn't.'

'Well, neither did I, but then, at a guess I'd say no one did,' he surmised. 'Doubtlessly she'd heard we've hardly been on speaking terms for a couple of days— certainly it wouldn't take much for the information to make the rounds, an unthinking word in passing by anyone on the property would probably be sufficient— and she's just made her own deductions from there, being only too aware that, with a face and figure like yours, my love,' he touched his fingers to her smooth cheek softly, 'it isn't likely there's a man alive who *wouldn't* want to make love to you.'

'Except you, apparently,' in an unknowingly desolate tone.

'You think not?' Slade's grey eyes darkened explicitly as they locked with hers. 'Hell, it nearly killed me *not* to make love to you that night!'

'Then wh-why didn't you?' she forced herself to ask, albeit with a self-conscious falter she was unable to control. It was a question that had often intruded upon her thoughts since that evening. 'You know I w-wouldn't have stopped you, and your rejection would have had an even more devastating effect if you'd waited until—until afterwards, wouldn't it?'

'And I suspect that's precisely the reason I didn't!

Because although I kept telling myself I was simply playing a role, subconsciously at least I think I must have known it was something else entirely and, therefore, just couldn't bring myself to actually carry out my original plan.' He shook his head in self-disgust. 'The only trouble being, I was too damned stubborn, and stupid, to realise the reason I wanted you so much was purely and simply because I loved you . . . not because of any idiotic thoughts of revenge I may have believed were still running around inside my head!'

'Although you do still believe I was in league with Luke, presumably?' she sighed despondently.

'I don't think I've really believed that for weeks,' he owned, heavily wry. 'I just continued trying to convince myself I did because otherwise I may have had to admit I was keeping you with me all the time for no other reason than that I liked it!' His mouth suddenly swept upwards disarmingly. 'And did so, more and more, as each day went by.'

Drawing in a deep breath, Taryn confessed pensively, 'I liked b-being with you too.'

'And now?' watchfully.

Her lower lip started to tremble and she caught at it with even white teeth. 'I told you once how I—I felt, but . . .'

'I ruthlessly, brainlessly, repulsed you,' Slade groaned regretfully. 'Can you ever forgive me?'

Taryn dropped her gaze to her tightly entwined fingers. 'If I could just be sure you really did l-love me, if only a little . . .' Her shimmering amethyst eyes lifted again, hesitantly.

Slade promptly pulled her close, his arms enfolding her reassuringly. 'Oh, honey, how could I have been so bloody insensitive as to reduce you to such an insecure state!' he castigated himself contemptuously. His arms tightened imperceptibly. 'But I swear I do love you, Taryn, and considerably more than a little, at that! In fact, I'd like nothing better than to spend the rest of my life proving to you just how much, if you'll let me!'

'I think I'd like that,' she murmured on a muffled note against his chest, taking her courage in both hands.

'What did you say?' he sought clarification intently as a hand beneath her chin tipped her face up to his.

Swallowing, she repeated with a nervously faint smile, 'I said, I think I'd like that.' But immediately added a protective, 'If you really did mean it, of course.'

'Oh, I meant it all right!' The very fervency of his tone was comfortingly convincing. 'And I'll start by marrying you as soon as can possibly be arranged.'

Regaining a little of her confidence, Taryn glanced upwards from beneath long, curling lashes. 'You can't think of some small thing that may be appropriate for right now?' she prompted winsomely.

A captivating smile spread across Slade's striking features, and she thought her heart would burst. '*I love you!*' he vowed in thickening accents, and crushing her to him possessively, claimed her willingly parting lips in a kiss that both delighted and shocked her with the intensity of emotion it conveyed and, in turn, aroused. When he at last raised his head again some long, exhilarating minutes later, Slade's breathing was as ragged as Taryn's. 'And I trust that assures you I have no intention of leaving you—*ever*—let alone at the church.' He smiled down at her crookedly.

With a contented sigh, Taryn remained happily

within the circle of his arms. 'And I hope *you* now know that it was only because I couldn't bear the thought of leaving you that I didn't accept Luke's money when he first offered it.' Her eyes suddenly sought his anxiously. 'You do believe that, don't you, Slade?'

'Mmm, I believe it,' he both smiled and nodded so reassuringly that she relaxed again. 'Although I can't say I'd complain if you should feel like explaining precisely why you couldn't bear to have left.' His eyes gleamed with gently teasing laughter.

'But you know why,' she evaded, doing a little tormenting of her own. Then relented and confessed deeply, 'Because I loved you then, I love you now, and will always love you till the day I die.'

Bending his head, he kissed her lingeringly. 'I don't deserve you.'

'Your mother may feel the shoe's on the other foot,' she half laughed ruefully.

'But I understood from when I was talking to her after Ilona's departure that she'd told you only this morning that she was in favour of you joining the family,' he frowned.

'Mmm, but that was before I—umm—let Ilona have one in the eye,' she reminded with an expressive grimace. 'And your mother doesn't exactly take to people who make scenes, remember?'

'Well, not in someone else's house, anyway,' he grinned. 'While at home ... well, she does prefer to have a little spirit about them and, in your case especially, I rather think she considers Ilona's misfortune could have been deserved.' He gave an utterly stirring laugh of remembrance. 'You might also be interested to learn that she informed me, in no uncertain terms, that I needed my head read if I still believed you were implicated in your brother's activities. Likewise, if I *didn't* marry you.'

'Oh!' Taryn flushed becomingly at such unexpected support, and then dimpled mischievously. 'That's right, you did say once that she was an extremely perceptive woman, didn't you?'

Instead of the equally bantering retort she had been anticipating, however, Slade merely smiled lazily. 'And how right I was!' he averred on a husky note as he lowered his head to hers once more.

Coming Next Month in Harlequin Romances!

2731   TEARS OF GOLD   Helen Conrad
The mystery man found panning for gold on a young woman's
California estate sparks her imagination—especially when she learns
he's bought her family home!

2732   LORD OF THE AIR   Carol Gregor
There's turbulence ahead when the owner of a flying school wants
to build a runway on his neighbor's land. He disturbs her privacy,
not to mention her peace of mind....

2733   SPRING AT SEVENOAKS   Miriam MacGregor
A young Englishwoman's visit to a New Zealand sheep station
arouses the owner's suspicions. No woman could be counted on to
live in such isolation! Why should she be any different?

2734   WEDNESDAY'S CHILD   Leigh Michaels
Is it generosity that prompts a man to offer his estranged wife money
for their son's medical expenses? Or is it a bid to get her under his
thumb again?

2735   WHERE THE GODS DWELL   Celia Scott
A fashion photographer abandons her glamorous career for an
archaeological dig in Crete. But she has second thoughts when she
falls in love...and clashes with old-world Greece.

2736   WILDERNESS BRIDE   Gwen Westwood
Concern brings an estranged wife to her husband's side on an
African wilderness reserve when blindness threatens him. But he
insists on reconquering the wilderness...and her!

Here's how to get this special offer from Harlequin!

As simple as 1…2…3!

1. Each month, save one Treasury Edition coupon from your favorite Romance or Presents novel.
2. In four months you'll have saved four Treasury Edition coupons (<u>only one coupon</u> per month allowed).
3. Then all you have to do is fill out and return the order form provided, along with the four Treasury Edition coupons required and $1.00 for postage and handling.

Mail to: Harlequin Reader Service

In the U.S.A.
2504 West Southern Ave.
Tempe, AZ 85282

In Canada
P.O. Box 2800, Postal Station A
5170 Yonge Street
Willowdale, Ont. M2N 6J3

RT1-D-2

Please send me my FREE copy of the Janet Dailey Treasury Edition. I have enclosed the four Treasury Edition coupons required and $1.00 for postage and handling along with this order form.

(Please Print)

NAME _____

ADDRESS _____

CITY _____

STATE/PROV. _____ ZIP/POSTAL CODE _____

SIGNATURE _____
This offer is limited to one order per household.

SUPPLIES LIMITED

This special Janet Dailey offer expires January 1986.

H·A·R·L·E·Q·U·I·N

FIRST·CLASS
Sweepstakes

OFFICIAL RULES

1. NO PURCHASE NECESSARY. To enter, complete the official entry/order form. Be sure to indicate whether or not you wish to take advantage of our subscription offer.

2. Entry blanks have been preselected for the prizes offered. Your response will be checked to see if you are a winner. In the event that these preselected responses are not claimed, a random drawing will be held from all entries received to award not less than $150,000 in prizes. This is in addition to any free, surprise or mystery gifts which might be offered. Versions of this sweepstakes with different prizes will appear in Preview Service Mailings by Harlequin Books and their affiliates. Winners selected will receive the prize offered in their sweepstakes brochure.

3. This promotion is being conducted under the supervision of Marden-Kane, an independent judging organization. By entering the sweepstakes, each entrant accepts and agrees to be bound by these rules and the decisions of the judges, which shall be final and binding. Odds of winning in the random drawing are dependent upon the total number of entries received. Taxes, if any, are the sole responsibility of the prize winners. Prizes are nontransferable. All entries must be received by August 31, 1986.

4. The following prizes will be awarded:

   (1) Grand Prize: Rolls-Royce™ *or* $100,000 Cash!
   (Rolls-Royce being offered by permission of
   Rolls-Royce Motors Inc.)

   (1) Second Prize: A trip for two to Paris for 7 days/6 nights. Trip includes air transportation on the Concorde, hotel accommodations…PLUS…$5,000 spending money!

   (1) Third Prize: A luxurious Mink Coat!

5. This offer is open to residents of the U.S. and Canada, 18 years or older, except employees of Harlequin Books, its affiliates, subsidiaries, Marden-Kane and all other agencies and persons connected with conducting this sweepstakes. All Federal, State and local laws apply. Void in the province of Quebec and wherever prohibited or restricted by law. Winners will be notified by mail and may be required to execute an affidavit of eligibility and release, which must be returned within 14 days after notification. Canadian winners will be required to answer a skill-testing question. Winners consent to the use of their name, photograph and/or likeness for advertising and publicity purposes in conjunction with this and similar promotions without additional compensation. One prize per family or household.

6. For a list of our most current prize winners, send a stamped, self-addressed envelope to: WINNERS LIST, c/o Marden-Kane, P.O. Box 10404, Long Island City, New York 11101

SWRL·A·1

Take 4 books
& a surprise gift
FREE

SPECIAL LIMITED-TIME OFFER

Mail to   **Harlequin Reader Service**®

In the U.S.   In Canada
2504 West Southern Ave.   P.O. Box 2800, Station "A"
Tempe, AZ 85282   5170 Yonge Street
                                  Willowdale, Ontario M2N 6J3

YES! Please send me 4 free Harlequin Romance® novels and my
free surprise gift. Then send me 6 brand-new novels every month as
they come off the presses. Bill me at the low price of $1.65 each
($1.75 in Canada)—a 11% saving off the retail price. There are no
shipping, handling or other hidden costs. There is no minimum
number of books I must purchase. I can always return a shipment
and cancel at any time. Even if I never buy another book from
Harlequin, the 4 free novels and the surprise gift are mine to
keep forever.

Name _____ (PLEASE PRINT)

Address _____ Apt. No. _____

City _____ State/Prov. _____ Zip/Postal Code _____

This offer is limited to one order per household and not valid to present
subscribers. Price is subject to change.   DOR–SUB–1